PRAISE FOR JEFF BURK

"Like Lloyd Kaufman and Sam Raimi's mutant offspring."

-Wil Wheaton

"If Chuck Klosterman raised a child on Jack Kerouac, Star Trek and comic books, that kid would be Jeff Burk. Original stuff that is sure to turn heads for fans of any literary genres."

-MC Lars

"Jeff Burk writes some awesome shit. Just read it."

-Carlton Mellick III

"Jeff Burk watches too much TV."

-Chester Knebel, head animator for SUPERJAIL Season 1.

"Reminiscent of a modern William Faulkner."

-Lloyd Kaufman, President of Troma Entertainment and creator of The Toxic Avenger

T0272772

THE VERY INEFFECTIVE HAUNTED HOUSE

AND OTHER STRANGE & STUPID STORIES

JEFF BURK

Copyright © 2018 by Jeff Burk

Cover by Joel Amat Güell

ISBN: 978-1-944866-16-7

CLASH Books

PO BOX 487 Claremont, NH 03743

CONTENTS

THE VERY INEFFECTIVE HAUNTED HOUSE

I AM THE HOUSE.

I haunt this house.

These two things are the same. I really can't explain the physics or philosophy of it so I'm going to have to ask you to just go with this.

I don't have a name and I don't know how I got here. I do know that at some point I was alive but I only have the vaguest memories of it. They are just brief flashes of what I was before. It's like trying to remember what happened after a night of heavy drinking. I know I was a man and I know I wanted to be an artist.

I don't know if I was black or white, tall or short, rich or poor, religious or atheist.

This is what I look like now.

I never said I was a good artist, just that I wanted to be one.

When I died I ended up here. I don't know who, how, or why I haunt this house, just that I'm suppose to.

I think about my death a lot. I wonder how I died. I hope it wasn't drowning, burning, or being crushed. They all seem like shitty ways to go. I hope I had a sudden brain aneurysm right after orgasm when fucking my beautiful wife who loved me as deeply as I loved I her. That's what I like to think my life was like while I was on the human plane. I like to imagine that it was filled with joy, love, and hope.

I spend a lot of time making up stories to myself—of adventures and romances that I had while alive. I do this because I am alone. No one lives in me but a few rats. Use to scare them as they crept around looking for cockroaches to eat by slamming doors and cupboards. I stopped doing that because I got bored. There's no challenge to star-tling mice. They look like this when they are terrified.

There's another haunted house down the street. We used to talk sometimes. We could communicate in a way that does not involve words, just reaching with our energies. Don't think about it too much, it's a haunted house thing.

I say used to, because the house was a fucking asshole. It was always a jerk to me calling me names like 'soyboy' and 'cuck.' I don't even know what those word mean but I could tell from the way it said them that I was supposed to be insulted.

It called itself the 'God of Hungry Walls.' What a pretentious asshole. And it would tell me the vile things that it did to the humans in its walls. Awful thing. Terrible things.

But it did seem good at being a haunted house. The things it did were really scary.

It was also a writer. It even got a novel published by some press out of Portland that specialized in sex and violence. It seems trashy to me but if that jerk could get published maybe I could still be an artist.

Here's what it looked like.

So now I spend my days practicing my art in the attic. My only company are the rats who sometimes stop by and watch me draw. They sit, fascinated, as I draw sunsets and boats in the thick layers of dust.

I sometimes feel bad that I was mean to them.

A family moved into me. A husband and wife in their early thirties with a young daughter of around five or six.

They look like this.

I watched them unload their belongings in cardboard boxes and place them all throughout me. I was enraptured, it had been so long since I saw people. They were so full of brightness and happy emotions. I saw the husband steal a quick kiss from the wife, both of them sweaty and dirty from moving into me. That love, that kindness, it felt so foreign. It's been so long since I felt anything like that.

And there's something else. They have a future. A weird aura that shows that they are still moving forward in time while I exist outside of it. I lost time and the boundless potential that comes with having a future so very long ago.

It makes me sad.

OK, showtime.

Their first night inside of me I'm not really sure what to do. I guess this is my job but I really wish there would have been some training.

I could do the whole banging doors and cupboards thing but it seems like I should try harder on people.

What about spooky sounds?

I vaguely remember horror movies. Those are a still a thing, right? Ghosts would play music on a piano and when someone would show up to investigate, the room would always be empty.

I went to the living room and looked around but there was no piano. There were no musical instruments of any kinda.

Singing also happens in those movies, I think. I haven't been around humans for so long that it's hard to remember all the details.

I wrack my consciousness for music.

I found something buried deep.

Now it was just a matter of finding my voice again.

"S…S…Some."

Wow. I didn't expect my voice to sound like that. I mean, I didn't know what I was expecting but not that.

"Somebody once told me…"

I paused and waited to hear any movement from above in the bedrooms.

Nothing.

"The world is gonna roll me…"

I waited again.

A creek came from above and then the sounds of footsteps.

I ain't the sharpest tool in the shed…"

The footsteps are moved out of the room and into the hallway.

"She was looking kinda dumb…"

The steps were coming down the stairs.

"With her finger and her thumb…"

Now they were just around the corner.

"In the shape of an L…"

Now the husband was in the doorway and I went silent. He flipped on the overhead lights.

His face was…confused. He didn't look scared at all. If anything, I'd say he look annoyed.

He looked around the room and flipped off the lights. He turned to leave.

Shit! I had to give it one more go.

"On her forehead!" I shouted.

He stopped and turned around. The lights came back on.

He stepped into the room looking around more carefully this time. But he still looked annoyed more that any sort of fear.

"What the fuck," he muttered to himself as he began to look around at the many boxes that were all over the room.

The wife came down the stairs and into the room, wrapping herself in a purple robe.

"What the hell was that?" she said sounding a bit pissed.

"It sounded like Eric Andre singing Smash Mouth," said the husband.

"Who?"

"Never mind. Your phone's upstairs, right?"

"Yeah, next to yours."

"What about your laptop or tablet?"

"Upstairs also, what about your stuff?"

"In the office. I was just setting them up before bed."

"What about speakers, are they in any of the boxes?"

"I...don't think so but I'm not completely certain. But what would they even be plugged in to?"

"I don't know but I'm not hearing it anymore."

"Me neither," he said walking over to her.

"Let's worry about it tomorrow. I want to go back to sleep."

They walked away and I watched them go.

That did not go as planned.

I decided I wasn't going to beat myself up over this. It's my first haunting after all. There's a learning curve to everything. I can't be expected to kick ass on my first try. I must learn and improve from experience.

I observed them for a few days. I watched them unpack their belongings and continue their routines of life—their work, school, and hobbies.

I didn't learn a fucking thing.

It was time to change my strategy. I needed to work from outside myself. I had to think bigger.

We haunted houses can do all sorts of crazy stuff that is hard to explain to humans but it just comes naturally. I reached out into the surrounding world to find and attract the most dangerous and vicious predator within my reach. The best way I could describe the feeling of doing that to you is it's like a controlled sneeze.

I felt something but I didn't know what it was. I could feel that it had taken many lives and was feared among the local wildlife.

I pulled the beast to the house and I could feel it coming closer and closer until it came right up my front door.

It looked like this.

It was a cat.

Like I said, it's hard to "see" anything outside of myself. I had been wondering where I was. If a cat was the most dangerous beast nearby it couldn't be that bad of an area.

The cat looked up at me and purred.

It was kinda cute.

It kept purring and scratched at the door.

No, kitty, don't do that!

Kitty kept purring and scratching.

The door opened and it was the daughter. She squealed in delight at seeing the fluffy cat.

The cat leapt into her arms and she squealed even louder. She turned around and ran into the house yelling, "mommy, mommy!"

OK, attempt number two ended with the family getting a pet. Looking at the positives of this, I have at least done something that will have a lasting effect. The first time I only caused a minor annoyance but this time the effects will be long lasting. The effects maybe love and companionship with a furry friend but it's still long lasting. I just have to fine tune my focus.

I've been watching the family. They seem happy. The kitty likes to purr at me.

I decided to go cheap and bang the doors and cupboards at night. All I succeeded in doing was getting the cat in trouble. It turns out it's really hard to haunt a house when there's a cat running around at night.

Singing songs also failed on repeated attempts. Once they had all their electronics set up all my singing earned was some annoyed late night calls to customer service for their products.

My strategies were not working.

I observed them live their lives but I also spent a lot of time in the attic working on my drawings with the rats watching. They didn't like to leave the attic much anymore since the cat moved in. I think I'm getting a bit better at my art.

Here's a fish.

There was lots of space for me to work with in the attic, as it was a full floor and the room was completely bare. The family didn't even know there was an attic. Someone had painted over the edges of the pull down ceiling stairs on the second floor long before I was ever here.

I liked having my own space.

One night I was watching the husband and wife sleep and I got a strange tingle. It's hard to explain since you have a body but it felt like a tickle in your kidney—but a sexy kind of tickle in your kidney.

And then I moved the wife's left index finger. It was just a little bit but I moved it.

I raised her arm into the air and then gently put it back down on the bed.

Then I made her stand up.

I was so excited. I had complete control of her. I could make her do anything.

I looked at her eyes and they were still shut. Despite the sudden hijacking of her body she was still fast asleep.

I took her to the door and had her carefully and quietly open it. She stepped through and shut it in near silence. I took her downstairs but made sure to make every step soft as possible. I was taking every precaution to not wake the husband or daughter.

I took her to the kitchen. There I began to feel urges. Urges I cannot describe. Just like people have unexplainable drives to laugh, cry, and have sex, haunted houses have similar primal feelings. I'm just not sure what they mean yet. This was all new to me.

In the kitchen these drives became stronger and stronger. I

started thinking dark things, bad things, thing I never thought about before.

I could make her pick up the meat tenderizer. The cat was sleeping on the living room couch. We could make a nice messy red surprise for the daughter.

In the drawer were matches and lighter fluid for the outside barbecue. We could take them upstairs, spray the husband with the fluid, and set his face on fire before he even knew what was happening.

Or we could take the knife. The big one used for cutting up meat. We could go to the daughter first and then the husband and then the wife could slit her throat. They'd all be gone and I could just wait for the next family to come into my death trap.

We picked up the knife and walked upstairs. Careful to go slow and quiet. There wasn't a creak and not even the cat stirred.

We entered the daughter's room and looked down at her. She cuddled a pink teddy bear. She breathed in and out in the peaceful sleep that is only known to the young and the idiots.

We raised the knife.

The walls were covered with sheets of construction paper. Each one was a child's masterpiece made with finger paint, crayons, and markers. There were dragons, horses, monsters, and kittens.

I had been watching but not seeing these people.

I looked down at the daughter and for the first time I saw an artist.

A tear ran down the wife's face as I saw the daughter through her eyes. I saw her in ways I had never seen any of them before. I saw time stretch out like a tunnel, branching off into an infinite number of paths. All unknown and unseen even to me.

And I could sever them all.

I wouldn't be taking a life. I'd be taking a multitude of possibilities and I would be destroying the ties to billions and billions of other humans they cross with.

We couldn't do it.

We lowered the knife.

We left the room and went down the stairs into the kitchen, each step soft and quiet to not disturb any living thing. We put the knife back and went back up to the bedroom. We lay down and I exited her body.

The moment I left the wife's body she bolted awake—screaming and weeping.. The husband woke up and started consoling her, assuring her that she just had a nightmare, but she kept sobbing, terrified.

The next morning when she was in the shower, I waited until she turned off the water. I went in and wrote a message to her in the fogged glass of the mirror.

I left before she pulled aside the shower curtains. I didn't want to be there when she read it.

I felt...something I don't like.

The message said: I'm sorry.

I had only watched them before but now I finally saw them. I saw their lives. The beautiful boringness of it all. The repetition of life. Eat, sleep, and occupy the rest of the time with ritual and tradition. They clean, work, laugh, fight, and cry. I don't understand most of it but I watch it.

The rats in the attic watched me drawing the things I saw, but they were not the same rats I knew before. They were different but yet still the same. It was their grandchildren. Yet they still came to watch me.

One day I was watching the wife cooking in the kitchen. The house was empty except for her, the kitty, and the rats. The daughter was sleeping over at a friend's house for the night, the husband was working late, and the kitty was hunting bugs outside.

I watched her slice vegetables and season meat and then she stopped. She turned her head and looked around and then she looked directly at me even though I held no form.

"I know you're there," she said.

I had no idea what to do.

She looked down and then back up at me.

"Thank you," she said. Tears began forming at the corners of her eyes. "Thank you for not making me do it."

I left the kitchen and hid in the attic. Something was happening to me that I had never experienced before. Something that was unknown to me as a haunted house. Something that shook me in in such a way that all I could do was hide in the attic with my pictures.

I felt guilty.

I didn't come back down. I just stayed with the rats and drew pictures.

I don't know how long I had been up there when I started hearing noises from the staircase door.

"I think it's an attic," said the husband.

"An attic?" answered the wife.

They found my space.

They talked more but I couldn't hear it over the scraping sounds as the seal that protected me was roughly torn away. Soon they would be up here and my pictures that showed their lives, conversations, and whispered dreams covered every inch of space etched in the dust.

I could wipe the room clean. It would take just an instant. I knew that's what I should do but I just could not do it. I had spent too my time making the art and the pictures were all I had.

Then the stairwell cracked open and the ladder was pulled down. The rats scurried off to hide in the walls.

The husband and wife came up with flashlights. Each of their steps was a booming assault upon my space. I was the house but they infested it. They live in me but were not parasites or symbionts. They infested me. This space was my final solace and it was being invaded.

"We have an attic?" said the husband as he came up. "How long have we lived here and didn't know?"

"Five years," said the wife behind him. "I never noticed this either."

Five years? They've been in me that long?

The husband came into the attic and shined his flashlight around.

"Jesus fuck," he whispered.

The wife followed up and flashed her light around and gasped.

They saw their history since entering the house drawn crudely (I've come to terms with my ability) in the floor and angled walls that formed the roof.

"What in the absolute fuck," said the husband as he took it all in. Scenes of the family game nights, of the daughter painting, and the kitty playing.

The wife was quiet as she looked around.

"Was...is someone up here, watching us?" said the husband. He sounded scared. More scared than I ever made him.

"No," said the wife. "Look, they cover the floor there's no footsteps."

"This is terrifying," he said.

She flashed the light around, seeing all the happy, mundane, and pointlessly sad moments that I had captured.

"No," she said. "It's beautiful."

"Let's just go downstairs, paint over the stairs again and forget about it."

He started to say something to protest but she stopped him.

"Trust me," she said.

And he did. I could feel it. He had his doubts but he really did trust her.

As the headed back down she took one final look around the attic and I wrote a message to her over the top of a dinner scene.

Thank you, I wrote.

Her eyes stopped on it and she stared. Then she smile faintly and went down the stairs.

Later I could hear them painting back over the stairs that led up to my space.

They live and I watch them.

They lived the clichés of life. I don't remember my own but I know this, it doesn't make it any less touching knowing this is how every person lives. I witness the wife, husband, daughter, and kitty have their own trip through mortality.

I've become closer to them and I find myself having feelings for them. Good feelings. You may expect me to talk about love but haunted houses do not feel love. It's something different but it's still positive. I'm still new to all of this.

The closer I become to them the further I can see outside myself. I assumed my house was alone but I am in a city. There's so much around me from other houses to playgrounds, bodegas, bars, and government buildings. They all have their own voices but I do not speak their languages yet.

I watched the family as they went to work, school, and hunted and I learned I could do more.

The husband was walking back to his car after work when a man was following him. I could feel greed and desperation from him. He was going to do something bad and take from the husband. The man was stalking him in the city after dark and I pushed a trash can into him, sending him staggering into the street right into the path of an oncoming bus. His skulls was crushed beneath the wheels.

There was another man in the neighborhood that became infatuated with the wife. He lived somewhere nearby and would see her at the grocery store and I could feel lust from him. He followed her back to me in his car and waited outside. Once he was sure she was the only one home he came around to the back of the house. He was going to come inside and do bad things.

He was looking in a back window when I turned the ground to

liquid. He went under and I used every root from the trees to the grass to tear him apart and spread him around my ground.

The gardens bloomed and were fruitful the next spring.

The daughter remained shy and was bullied for always drawing pictures. One boy that tortured her the most brought a knife to school. He had bad plans for her. His daddy did bad things to him and he needed some way to let it out and he decided to let it out on her.

When the boy went to the bathroom between classes I hit him with the stall's door. He fell forward into the toilet bowl I snapped down the seat holding his head in place. I backed up the pipes and water, piss, and shit flowed up into his face, down his throat, and into his lungs. Eventually he stopped moving.

One day kitty was outside for a bug hunt when a starving coyote caught kitty's scent. It saw a easy meal and charged. Kitty was dumb and didn't see it coming. I went inside the coyote and crushed every organ. It fell to ground dead and blood and viscera spewed out from every orifice.

I don't know who my family was before but I know who my family is now.

As they branched out in life I branched out with them. Soon the daughter will be going to college and I will go with her. The wife and husband will stay in me and I will always be with them. Kitty does not have long for the mortal plane. The people don't know but there is something growing in kitty. Something devoid of all life and light that will consume her. When her time ends, kitty will join me and I won't be alone.

I still make pictures in dust in my attic. I've had to wipe away old ones to make space for the new ones. I don't think I'm getting any better but I still keep trying. I have eternity so trying is all that matters. Maybe, one day, one of my pictures will be really good.

I draw and the rats still watch me but I no longer feel lonely.

I am the house.

I haunt this house.

And this is my family.

THE WINDOW SHOULDN'T BE THERE

I WAS outside watering the plants, specifically the hop vines that climbed all over the front porch, when I noticed a window that should not exist.

It had been a hot summer day and we hadn't had rain in what seem like three months. This year was especially extreme for a dry spell. The plants needed to be watered on an almost daily regiment or else their leaves would begin to droop and wilt.

The hot pepper plants that filled the backyard had already been attended to along with the sunflowers that lined the side of the house and that just left the hop vines and the front yard patch of watermelons and pumpkins. The pumpkins and watermelons, after several months had barely grown beyond twigs. At this point in the season there was almost no chance that anything was going to happen with them. I had watered and fed the plants with fish fertilizer. Their lack of success wasn't due to my lack of trying. At least I didn't think it was. I was beginning to wonder if there was something wrong with the ground itself. That the soil was drained of nutrients. It was something I'd have to account for next season with compost.

The hops were doing OK. Not great. There weren't enough cones to brew beer but you could pick them and drop them in your drink to give a nice fresh hop flavor. I'd also have to attend to that plot for the next year.

Watering always seemed to take much longer than it should. The water never seemed to flow right out of the hose. I don't know if it was the hose itself or the sprayer. The flow was never as strong or consistent as it should be—it was like a weak shower head. It was yet one more thing I needed to look into.

On the positive side this made watering the plants the perfect time to get really stoned and listen to podcasts. I was listening to an old episode of Last Podcast on the Left about the Toy Box Murders —my favorite serial killer story that no one seems to talk about— and my mind was wandering when I noticed that something was wrong.

The house I lived in was your standard two story Portland home. A mostly unremarkable house painted white with blue highlights around the windows and door frame. The paint was weathered and chipped from years of rain. The roof was brown and falling apart. It was not an uncommon occurrence to find shingles in the yard after a particularly heavy rain. This had been brought up to the landlord in the past but he'd never taken any action to fix it. Just like he never acted on any issues with the dishwasher, the washing machine, or the furnace.

There are some benefits to having an absentee landlord. You can throw parties whenever you want, have people crash on your couch for months or have more pets than your lease allows. But it also means that if anything goes wrong it's up to you to fix it. The roof was well beyond our means and skill so nothing would happen with that until the roof itself collapses during a particularly strong storm —drenching or crushing my housemates that live on the second floor. Luckily, my cat and I live on the first.

Occasionally my girlfriend and I talked about buying the house. We loved the property—plenty of space with four bedrooms and a large backyard with a giant apple tree, fire pit, and plenty of space for me to grow dozens of hot pepper plants all while being in the heart of Portland. But there's no way we could ever afford it. She worked at a rich person's cat hotel—like a kennel but without no cages. Each cat with its own room. The cost people paid for their cats to stay there was more than my rent but she only got a little over minimum wage. I worked at a warehouse assembling DIY gardening and cooking kits—the kind of things that are only bought as gifts for the person that you don't know what to get.

At first it was just the abstract notion that something wasn't right. That something was different about the house. There was no new paint job and the roof wasn't falling apart any more than normal. Then it struck me—where the second story should have two front-facing windows there were now three.

The window on the left was to my girlfriend's room. Yes, we had separate bedrooms. No statement on our relationship. We both enjoyed having our own space and our schedules don't exactly match up with myself preferring very late nights and her enjoying waking before noon. The window on the right was to one of our house-mate's room (the only way to afford rent in this city to have several housemates and we had three).

Between those two windows was now a third. It looked just like the other two but it had never been there before.

As previously mentioned, I was stoned, so my first thought was that I was having one of those weed-induced brain farts. The kind of thing that leads to the stupid stoner stereotype. But have a few moments of starring up I knew that was not the case.

My second thought was that the landlord must have done some sort of renovation that I was unaware of but I quickly dismissed that. Construction as heavy as knocking a hole in the walls and installing a new window is something I would have assuredly noticed even if I was in a drunken coma from a late night/early morning horror movie and beer binge.

So where did that window come from?

I turned off the hose and stood in the front yard regarding this peculiar change.

Obviously I needed to figure out this mystery. I went inside through the front door and up the stairs to the second floor. In the upstairs hallway there were two doors—one to my girlfriend's room and the other to my housemate's. There wasn't some extra room that I had somehow completely forgotten about. This mysterious third window was in-between the two bedrooms. The geography of the house allowed a space between the two rooms but at best the space would have been standard insulation—definitely not large enough for some sort of unnoticed or forgotten room.

I went down the stairs and back outside to the front yard to confirm what I thought I saw. Sure enough, that third window that should not be there was still there.

Now a new explanation was entering my head. Perhaps I was suffering some sort of subtle and especially boring mental break-down. Where others had visions of reptilian overlords or conspiracies about child sex-trafficking being run out of pizzerias, my mind was reconstructing basic architecture. Outside of some ongoing issues with bouts of depression I had never suffered from any mental illness previously. Back in my college days I did take a lot of acid but this didn't seem like some sort of weird flashback.

A third party confirmation was needed.

I went back inside, up the stairs, and knocked on my girlfriend's door.

"Yeah?" she said from inside.

I opened the door on she was laying on her bed reading a book with a cover illustration of a fire-breathing dragon—one of those fantasy epics that she adored but I always found cheesy. Cuddled up around her were four of the cats. Between the two of us we owned five cats. Yeah, we're "those people." Four of them were always hanging out with her and the fifth was my fat lazy fuck of a cat that barely ever left my room. We never set out to have so many cats but that's another story.

"What's up?" she asked looking up from the book.

"Can you come outside with me?" I asked. "I want you to take a look at something."

"What is it?"

"It's…can you just come out with me? I want to get your take on something."

"OK," she said slightly confused and slightly annoyed as she closed her book.

We went out to the front yard and I turned towards the house.

"You notice anything different?" I asked.

Her eyes narrowed as the studied our home looking over the structure and the garden plots.

"No," she said slowly, not understanding what I was getting at.

"Really?" I said. "Nothing seems different to you?"

"No," she said still staring at the house.

Fuck. I could still plainly see the window. How do you tell someone you love that you are beginning to have a break in reality and that it is manifesting itself in hallucinatory building renovations?

I was searching for some way to confess this when she gasped. Her eyes went wide and I could tell that she was looking at the exact spot with the new mystery window.

"What the fuck," she muttered more to herself than to me.

"You see it, right?" I asked, jubilant for some sort of confirmation. "The window."

"Yeah," she said nodding. "Where the hell did that come from?"

"Oh, thank god. I was beginning to wonder if I was losing it."

"No, no," she said, now moving around the yard to take the window in from different angles. "I see it too."

"That wasn't there before, right?"

"Nope."

"So what the fuck? How did we gain an extra window?"

"Did the landlord do something?"

"Not that I'm aware of. I'd think someone in the house would have noticed if that happened."

"Do...do we have a new room?"

"I just checked upstairs. Nothing that I could find."

"It would nice if we did. Could rent it out and lower everybody's rent."

She was the practical one in the relationship. I could barely manage my money to pay the bills while she successfully juggled multiple credit cards.

We went inside and confirmed together that there were no new room additions. We went back outside and stood next to each other staring up at the mysterious window.

"So what do we do?" I asked.

"Let's have a look in," she said. Her eyes never moving from the window. "Let's get the ladder."

We went around the back of the house to the back door that led down into the basement. We went down and got the twelve foot ladder that up until this point had solely been use to trim the trees and gigantic buses that lined the property.

We carried it to the front of the house and leaned it up to the window, taking care not to damage any of the hop vines with the base of the ladder.

"I'm going up," she said. "Can you hold the ladder steady for me?"

"Yep."

I stood at the bottom, holding the ladder as she climbed up. She went up slower than I expected. She was playing it cool but I could tell there was some nervousness to her. Something in the back of brain, in the primordial lizard part, began to panic and I knew she was feeling the same thing.

Finally, after what seemed like hours but was really just seconds, she got to the top and looked into the window.

"What can you see?" I shouted up.

"Nothing," she said. "It's dark. Really dark."

She cupped her hands around her eyes to better see whatever was inside when, with surprising speed and force, the window slid up and slammed open. She had been attempting to peer in from the upper half which place the open portion right at her waist.

From my vantage point I saw the window open but whatever could be inside was blocked from my view. I could only see a small bit of pure pitch blackness.

What happened next took place in just an instant but in my shock, time slowed down to where it was like a movie playing in slow motion.

———

She still had her hands cupped around her eyes as three arms reached out of the darkness. They were skinny and long—too long for any normal human. Each arm was at least five feet if not longer, and the skin was a pale alabaster white. They wrapped around her waist like snakes clutching onto fresh prey.

After seizing her they pulled back into whatever was on the other side of the window. She slammed hard into the window and the whole front the house shook. There was a loud cracking sound like a tree branch breaking in a wind storm.

Her body folded in half, but in a direction no human could bend, her heels almost touching the back of her head like a boneless ragdoll and then she disappeared through the open space. The window slammed shut behind her.

I was frozen in shock at the base of the ladder. I screamed her name. I climbed up the ladder as quickly as I could but didn't move fast enough. My limbs felt weighed down by the dread of what I was going to find.

On the other side of the window, there was an unnatural blackness. Normally if one is looking into a dark room one can tell that there is space and depth but I couldn't perceive any of that. There was only blackness, as if space and physicality did not exist on the other side. As if someone had hung a black curtain on the other side of the window but that's not even quite right as one would be able to perceive some texture of the cloth blocking the outside world.

It was just pure nothingness.

I reached down to the bottom of the window to try and open it, but there was nothing really to grab ahold of, as windows are not generally meant to be opened from the outside.

I pressed my palms against the glass to try and shove the frame up but, even with all my strength, it didn't budge in the slightest.

It was then that I noticed that the window was painted shut. Even though I had just seen the window open and shut, around all the edges were caked on layers of old paint.

This left me only one option—breaking the window.

I scurried down the ladder and ran to the back yard fire pit. It was something a previous occupant of the house had built. They had dug about a foot into the ground and then built up around the shallow hole with concrete bricks.

I wrenched one of the bricks out of the DIY creation and raced back around to the front of the house. I gripped the brick tightly in my hands as I ran. So tight that I could feel jagged imperfections leaving tiny cuts in my skin but I didn't care.

But when I came back to the front of the house, to the ladder that led up to that window, I froze. It had been an extremely pleasant

Portland late-summer day with temperatures in the mid-eighties but I was suddenly overtaken with a freezing cold sensation as if I had somehow stepped into a walk-in meat freezer.

The ladder was still there, propped up against the house and leading up to the second story. The ladder my girlfriend and I had set up together to investigate the mysterious window. The ladder she climbed up and then was pulled violently away from me. The ladder I myself had climbed to get her back.

The ladder was there but the window was gone.

It was just...gone. The ladder now just lead up to an unremarkable section of paneling.

I looked up trying to make sense what I was seeing—something I had been failing at all day. As I tried to wrap my brain around this the brick I holding, the brick I was going to use to smash that mysterious window and gallantly rescue my beloved, slipped from my fingers and fell to the ground.

I never saw her again.

I'm not really sure what happened next. In retrospect I now know that I was suffering from some level of shock. I don't know how long I stood out there staring up at the spot where the window had previously been. I do know that when I finally moved the sun was much lower in the sky than the start of all this.

I went inside and knocked on the door of one of my housemates —the one that shared the first floor with me. It's funny—not in a LOL kinda way but in a WTF kinda way—that I don't remember that housemate. I know they were a woman and someone I had known for quite some time in my life but while recording these events I cannot conjure her face, our history, or anything else about her.

I do remember frantically describing the events that I have related to you and taking her outside. She confirmed the ladder was there and she confirmed that it led to no window but there was zero evidence to the rest of my story. She asked me if I had taken something. I understand that assumption by my days of hallucinogen are long past the weed I had smoked earlier was long out of my system either from the passage of time or sobering shock.

The next most likely explanation that she said, as I have already brought up, was that I was just going crazy. Just straight-up losing my shit. There was nothing I say or do to alley her of those concerns. But she went upstairs to check on my girlfriend and confirmed that she was not around.

She just assured me that my girlfriend must be out and that I should call or text her. Which I did to explore all options but I never heard anything back.

My housemates never took me seriously and I can't blame them. I was the crazy person talking about a window that didn't exist and about arms that were too long that had taken my girlfriend away.

It wasn't until several days had passed and my girlfriend had missed all her work shifts and was not responding to family, calls, and emails that anyone began to take me seriously. And by take seriously, I mean that's when everyone began to suspect that I had killed her.

It's always the significant other that is suspected first and I understand why—because more times than not, that's exactly what's happened. If you are going to be murdered, statistically speaking, you are most likely to be killed by the person you share a bed with. Let's be honest, we can all understand why.

I reported her disappearance to the police, but they did not believe my accounting of events. I know the story sounded unbelievable but it's what happened. As more people that knew and depended upon her in day to day life reported her disappearance, the authorities began suspecting me.

The police were able to enlist the help of her cell phone provider. The provider was able to confirm that she took no calls, sent no texts, or interacted with anyone online since the date I said she went missing, but there was still a live signal and that signal came from inside the house.

The first assumption was that I had tried to cover the "crime" by burying her in the basement or garden like John Wayne Gacy or John Christie. But after a thorough ransacking of the house and the digging up of the property (killing all my plants in the process) they found nothing. Half of all murders in the United States are never solved even if the police believe they are certain they know who did it. This case and I were just another stat to contribute to that number.

Eventually my housemates moved out. I don't blame them. Living in a house with a man suspected of murdering his girlfriend and getting away with it, plus all the resulting media attention, does not make for a peaceful living environment. They were replaced with others via Craigslist ads, with tenants who were either unaware or didn't care about the accusations leveled towards me. That's just a small benefit to living in a city with rapidly raising housing costs.

It was around then that the cats started disappearing. After my girlfriend's family had come to claim all her possessions (a rather awkward affair in which they refused to speak to me or even entertain my claims of innocence) all I had left of her were our cats. The house already had a strange history of animals dying or disappearing from it. Several previous housemates had moved in with perfectly healthy pets only to have them succumb to cancer or other serious diseases within months. Other pets had straight-up vanished.

The first cat was gone on a rainy day in January. I scoured the house and neighborhood for him and put up flyers. Nothing came of that other than one asshole who left a voicemail saying that they hoped he was eaten by a coyote.

The second was gone a week later and the third two weeks after that. I searched the house, looking for some hole in the walls or foundation allowing them to escape but found nothing of the sort.

The fourth was gone a month later.

That left just me and my obese cat alone in a house we shared with people who were essentially strangers.

She had been gone for a full year when I was outside watering the plants when I once again saw the window that should not exist. Just as suddenly as it had disappeared, along with the woman I loved, it had returned.

I stared up at it and considered my choices of action. I could call the police and wait for them, never averting my gaze from the window so it didn't suddenly disappear again on me. But I sincerely doubted they would take my call seriously enough to come and investigate. I could call her family and attempt to prove to them that what I had been claiming all along was accurate, but I also didn't believe they would be any more willing to believe.

After some careful consideration I went around the back of the house and down into the basement. I struggled to bring up the ladder by myself—its size and weight unruly for just one person, but I had to do this alone. With some effort and quite a bit of sweat, I managed to get into the front yard and propped against the house. Leading up to that window.

Before climbing, I went inside and recorded my entire account of these weird events.

My plan, as long as that fucking window is still there, is to climb that ladder with a hammer, smash the glass, and find out what's on the other side. When I climbed the ladder last time nothing happened to me. Maybe whatever is on the other side only wants one person at a time. Maybe whatever is on the other side doesn't even want or need me.

This time it doesn't have a choice.

Maybe something—anything will be different this time.

Maybe I will finally get some answers.

I doubt I will like them.

TEN SECRETS TO SURVIVAL CLICKERS DON'T WANT YOU TO KNOW – THEY REALLY HATE NUMBER SIX

Brax Valentine: Buzzfeed Senior Food Correspondent

Reporting from New York City aka The Edge of the End of the World

1: YOU GOT TO KEEP BUSY

The city is dying but at least our wifi is still strong.

This is Brax Valentine, your favorite food correspondent holed up in Buzzfeed headquarters. I'm here with entertainment critic Juniper Johnson and U.S. news correspondent Scarlet Hansen. When the clickers came out of the sea and began to rampage through the city the rest of Buzzfeed staff fled to get to loved ones and government organized safe houses.

I don't know how many made it but I don't have high hopes.

The three of us stayed. We decided that our best bet was just to stay put. I still don't know if we made the right decision or not.

We're on the top floor of the Chaplin Building in downtown New York. The designer was a bit of a survival nut and that is proving to be extremely beneficial to us right now. It was built with completely self-sustaining utilities based upon cutting edge technology that I won't even pretend to understand. But I don't need to—all I need to know is that we've got water, electricity, and, most important of all, internet.

Being on the top floor provides us with views of much of the city and I'll be honest—it doesn't look good out there. If you ever wanted to see people butchered in the streets, this is the place to be.

Leaving is not an option. The streets are filled with what everyone has dubbed "clickers." Not that we could leave even if we wanted to. The clickers managed to get in the building and, to the best of our knowledge, they have completely infested the lower floors. We can hear the clicking of their claws from inside the elevator shafts and at the doorway to the stairs. So far they have not figured out that we are here and hopefully they never do.

So while we are here, I'll be reporting and what we see and doing. I'll be giving you a first-hand glimpse into survival on the front lines. I know all my previous writing has been about such cutting edge topics as the best pork belly ramen and twelve unorthodox uses for avocado's but I believe I'm up to this challenge.

I know things seem dire out there so I want to leave you on some positives notes. We all got to see Trump dismembered on TV by a giant crab/lobster/scorpion monster—something many of us have been dreaming of for years. Run the Jewels dropped their latest, and sadly probably last, mix tape just a week before this all went to shit. They were scheduled to be performing in Miami when the swarms hit and nobody's heard or seen them since, so enjoy it. And, lastly, I just saw on YouTube that Beyonce is confirmed to be alive and well in Minneapolis. She's going to be performing a benefit concert for all of us trapped in the DMZ this coming Thursday. If Bey can make it, we all can!

Until next time. Stay safe.

2: OFFICE URBAN FORAGING IS THE HIP NEW WAY TO EAT

We ran out of real food yesterday. Not that there was much of it anyway. Just some leftover lunches in the kitchenette's fridge—some

Chinese, Indiana, and Thai—good stuff but we ate it all. There was also a few jars of pickles, kale chips, a few packets of ramen, and some jars of homemade Kombucha. Personally I can't stand the stuff. The shit always came across to me like drinking the backwash beer of someone with a serious upper respiratory infection.

However we are stocked up on free trade coffee and tea at least. Apparently the office manager always made sure that the staff never ran out of either. I don't blame them. I shudder to think what would have happened. No clicker could compare to a twenty-three year old English lit major going through a major caffeine withdrawn.

We searched through all the desks in the office and found some organic chocolate bars, a large bag of wasabi peas, five tins of pickled squid (who the fuck keeps that in their desk?) and three large bags of almonds.

Rationing is the only option. Every day the three of us spilt one tin of pickled squid and small sides of the rest of our forage. The variety of snacks keep the meals interesting. The squid is surprisingly good. A bit chewy and the texture was odd but it had a barbecue sauce that really made it work. With a sprinkle of crushed ramen it's really no different than something you'd get downtown at Gato. It's like having gourmet survival tapas.

To keep the hunger pains at bay we are drinking a shit ton of coffee and tea plus smoking a lot cigarettes.

Oh yeah, we found a shit ton of smokes. Almost every desk had an emergency pack for whenever their owner had needed to visit flavor town. One poor addicted bastard even had a full carton. For such a health conscious work place we all apparently really liked our smokes.

To pass the time we indulge in the other harvest from our office foraging—drugs. We got about an ounce of pre-rolled joints, a fat sack of nugs (and some pipes of course), after combing the many mini baggies there was about a quarter of coke, around twenty capsules of molly, a vial of liquid acid, an ounce of shrooms, and about an eight of meth. We even got a few needles with heroin. Juniper and Scarlet are adamant that they aren't interested in the meth or heroin. I'm thinking that depending on how long this shit show last that I'll be breaking into them. I've always been curious.

The lesson to take away here is make sure you've done a thorough search and inventory of your surroundings. Who knows what goodies you can find to get through the coming days, weeks, or…

Well, however fucking long this is going to last.

3: STAY CONNECTED TO YOUR FELLOW HUMAN

It's important to not lose touch with your fellow human. Reading your messages and comments of support really helps keep my spirits up while surrounded by monsters outside, as our food stash gets lower and lower.

I have been noticing that my view counts have been lower than normal. Either I'm boring or there's less of you out there. I never before in my life hoped that I was boring but I like to think big picture and in this situation I sincerely hope I am.

I've been playing a lot of board games with Juniper and Scarlet. The breakroom has a decent collection of classics. They really like RISK but I'll be honest, I never saw the appeal. For a game that's supposed to be about strategy it's really just a bunch of die rolls to see who gets the highest number.

Yes, I'm bitter that Venezuela managed to take down Mexico even though my forces had four times as many soldiers. I think when this all blows over I should do an article about the top board games that are full of shit.

I'm also convinced that Scarlet cheats at MONOPOLY. She always wants to be the banker and I'm immediately suspicious of anyone that *wants* to be an accountant in what is meant to be a fun pastime. I swear to God that if I catch her palming a hundred I'll feed her to the clickers myself.

That's my report for today—RISK, just like real war, is bullshit and MONOPOLY is just as prone to corruption as the real world capitalistic system.

4: ALWAYS KEEP A BLUNT OBJECT ON HAND

A clicker got in today.

They've been crawling on the outside of the building and occasionally they go across the windows on their way to the roof. I don't know if they are stupid or just have really poor vision but they never seemed to notice that we are in here.

I don't even think it saw us, I think we were just really unlucky.

We were playing a very heated match of CHUTES AND LADDERS and passing a joint around when one of the windows smashed and a clicker tumbled in. I'm not sure who was more surprised, us or the clicker that was just doing clicker stuff and now it suddenly found itself in a room with humans.

Those moments in your life when everything just goes completely to shit are so odd. That old cliché of how time just seems to stop is surprisingly accurate. I know it was just a moment but I'll forever have etched in my mind that clicker standing there and taking in its new surroundings.

The fuckers can really move when they want to. For something so big they are surprising graceful and agile. In just an instant it rushed across the room and snatched up Juniper. She didn't stand a chance. The monster tore her in half instantly. At least she didn't suffer. It happened so quickly that I not sure she had time to process what happened—at least I hope not.

Scarlet was frozen in place with shock and I don't blame her at all. I have no idea how I managed to act. My body and mind just went on autopilot. I grabbed the fire extinguisher from the wall and ran up to the clicker. It was busy eating Juniper and paid me no mind.

All it took was one blow right on top of its head. I must have been lucky and hit just the right spot because the extinguisher smashed right through the shell and crushed whatever excuse for a brain that thing had. The cracking sound the shell made was one of the most satisfying things I've heard in my life. The clicker's whole body shuddered and then collapsed to the floor, dropping the two halves of Juniper.

After the shock of what happened wore off Scarlet and I moved the pieces of Juniper out into the hallway. We considered throwing her out the window that the clicker fell in through but were worried that another clicker might see us and come in for a snack. I just hope that when she starts to smell, it doesn't draw any clickers from inside the building.

Then we dealt with the broken window. We didn't have a tarp or blanket to cover it so we stacked up some of the desks to create a barricade. It's not much and certainly would not prevent a clicker from getting in if it really wanted to but it provided some peace of mind.

So rest in piece to Juniper Johnson. (Haha—get it? Jesus, that even made me cringe. I think I've been up here for too long.) I didn't know her very well but she was a good movie critic. She may no longer be with us but she'll never have to watch another shitty DC Comics film again.

5: CONSIDER ALL OPTIONS NO MATER HOW DISTASTEFUL

Scarlet and I have two problem—we are now officially out of food and the clicker corpse is too big and heavy to move.

So I have an idea to take care of both problems.

The clickers look like a combination of crabs, lobsters, and scorpions and all three animals are things that people eat. It stands to reason then that we should be able to eat a clicker.

I proposed this idea to Scarlet but she is really not into it. She says that she's not interested in eating something that partially ate one of her co-workers. I said that it would be a fitting revenge.

Plus she says that she doesn't like seafood.

My plan is to use the fire extinguisher to break off the limbs and crack the shell. It's going to take some effort but I'm pretty sure I can do it.

I kind of intrigued about this venture. I've always been an adventurous eater and love dishes as varied as pickled pork lung and squirrel pot pie. To the best of my knowledge I'll be the first person to eat clicker meat and that alone excites me. Hell, my position here at Buzzfeed is to be a food writer. I almost feel like it's my professional duty to try this.

I'm going to go and get to work. I'll be reporting back soon.

6: CLICKERS TASTE PRETTY DAMN GOOD

My experiment was a success!

I decided that I would try a claw first. That's always been my favorite part of shellfish so it seemed like a good place to start.

We have a small stove in the kitchenette that I used to fry up the meat. Normally I wouldn't make seafood so well done but there's no telling what kind of parasites these things could be carrying. I've made it this far and it'd be a shame to go out by shitting my pants to death.

I'd compare the taste to lobster but a bit saltier and with a slight bitterness. The meat was stringier and tougher than what I was expecting, but that could be from how much I cooked it.

Overall I give it a positive ranking. I wish I had some butter or herbs to go with it but it is sure nice to eat something other than canned squid or dry snacks. It feels good to have a full belly again.

When this whole thing is over I bet we'll be seeing clickers on a lot of restaurant menus. With how much meat is in these things it could be a solution to world hunger.

No matter how bad things get you still have to try new things.

I think I'm going to try that meth next. It's something I've never tried and considering everything that's happened I think now is a good time.

7: METH IS REALLY FUCKING AWESOME

Seriously! This shit is great! I can't believe I haven't been doing it my entire life.

I offered Scarlet some but she was adamantly against it. That's fine. More meth for me.

I highly recommend it being a part of every survival kit.

8: DON'T BELIEVE EVERYTHING YOU READ

OK, I've been getting some concerned messaged from those of you that are also reading Scarlet's reports.

Despite what she's writing, under no circumstances have I been "eying her with feral hunger" nor have I been staying up all night watching her sleep, waiting for a "moment in which [her] guard is down to strike and feast."

I'll be honest, things are getting a bit desperate here. The clicker meat went bad fairly quickly—it only took about twelve hours before it went rancid. Even the pieces I put in fridge went bad. Scarlet and I moved the clicker parts out into the hallway with the halves of Juniper but we can still smell the rancid stench. Nothing is worse than the smell of rotting seafood. Now all we have to consume is water, coffee, tea, and the copious amount of drugs.

The combination wears on your mind as is evident from Scarlet's bouts of paranoia. I immensely respect all the hard work she's down at this company. Her reporting of the disaster in Phillisport was groundbreaking at a time when no one was taking the clickers seriously. And her pieces on the international implications of the fall of D.C. would have made Friedman proud. But, quite frankly, she wasn't ready to handle this kind of direct danger as she is no field reporter.

Her unfounded concerns about me are proof of this.

Now all of us left have to keep our heads if we are to have any hope of getting out of this alive.

And I mean all of us.

I'm seeing rumors on Reddit and Twitter that there are other monsters now coming out of the ocean behind the clickers. People are claiming that there are green scaly humanoid like things directing the clickers.

As of right now there is no firm proof of what have been dubbed "the Dark Ones" and I sincerely doubt that any will come. I understand why people are getting desperate. This is the same kind of logic that conspiracy theorists and religious nuts subscribe to—it's an innate trait in humans. When faced with something as horrible and random as the clickers we try to make sense of it. People want to believe that there is something in control of what is happening. It's easier than accepting that sometimes bad things happen and that when you get right down to it the world is in a perpetual state of chaos.

That's where we all are right now. Keep your head. Keep your cool.

9: OK, MAYBE YOU SHOULD BELIEVE WHAT YOU READ

Well, I was really fucking wrong.

Just a few hours after I last wrote you all I saw what people are calling the Dark Ones.

I was smoking a cig while standing at the windows tripping balls on some LSD and watching the buildings in the city burn (a beautiful and mind-blowing experience—like I said earlier, make the best of everything and try to have new experiences whenever you can) when I saw them in the streets below. At first I thought it was just a psychedelic trick of the eye but then I stopped peaking and I could still see them.

But I'm sure you don't need my confirmation. The videos are all over YouTube.

So there are now two types of monsters coming out of the ocean and invading. Isn't nature amazing!

Also, I killed Scarlet.

Believe me, I didn't want to do it but it was the only responsible option. I've been reading her posts and her paranoia just kept getting stronger and stronger. If I didn't get her it was only a matter of time before she got me.

Ever read something online that got you so enraged that you just wanted to kill the person that wrote it? Let me tell you, it feels really fucking good to do it.

I waited until she fell asleep, smoke some meth, and crept up on her with the fire extinguisher. I bashed her in the head just like I did with the clicker but it took Scarlet about a dozen blows before she finally went still.

I've also been eating her. I don't have a proper knife for the job but a sharp piece of clicker shell has been doing a decent enough job. I've been cutting hunks out of her and frying them up. You know those stories of cannibal tribes calling humans "long pig?" It's true. We really do taste like pork.

10: NEVER GIVE UP—UNLESS THAT IS THE BEST OPTION

My hits on these blogs have gone way down. I guess you all out there aren't doing too well.

In other bad news there are now giant monsters in the city. Clickers that are several stories tall are smashing buildings to the ground.

I wonder if clickers are like lobsters in that the older they are the bigger they are. If so, these ones must be hundreds if not thousands of years old. And one of those big fucks is headed my way.

For the first time since this all began, I seriously think that it's not going to be OK. I don't think I'm getting out of this.

To add insult to injury, I'm completely out of meth.

I've started to use the heroin. It makes you feel really good—it's what I imagine fucking an angel must be like. Honestly, I'm more of a meth guy (never thought I'd say that). But combined with some of the acid or molly or both, it's still pretty satisfying.

So this is what I'm going to do—once I'm done with this entry I'm going to take as many of the drugs that I can. Shoot up the rest of the heroin, pop all the molly, chug the acid—I'm gonna do it all. Then I'm going to go to sleep and just never wake up.

Thanks everyone for being here with me through this shit show. I wish you all the best of luck. If you happened to be stumbling onto this posts after I'm gone I hope some of my tips help you make it through this terrible situation we all find ourselves in.

You know how all those Lovecraft stories end with the narrator encountering some horrible evil or monster and ending their journal entries with the implication that they are going to die? This is just like that.

From Buzzfeed in New York City, this has been Brax Valentine.

Signing off.

HOW I GOT A MY LITTLE PONY
TATTOO

"Here," said Ezra rolling up his sleeve. "Take a fucking look at this."

"Holy shit," said Megan, squinting in the bar's dim light. "Is that… Barney the Dinosaur?"

"Yep, it is," said Ezra as he looked down at the purple blob tattooed on his bicep.

"Where'd you get it? They didn't do a very good job on it," said Ed. "The lines aren't straight at all."

Ezra sighed. "No, they didn't." He rolled down the sleeve, covering the embarrassing piece.

"Guys," he said. "I think I have inkers."

"Oh shit," said Megan.

"Inkers? I didn't even know they were real," said Ed. "I thought they were just a phrase, from that children's rhyme."

"No, they're real," said Megan. "I have some friends in New York that got them."

"I wasn't sure at first," said Ezra. "I thought maybe the *Power Rangers* thing was just a drunken decision—"

"—what *Power Rangers* thing?" said Ed.

"I didn't show you?"

"No."

"Oh shit, check this fucker out."

Ezra lifted his leg onto the table and rolled up his pants. On his left calf was a black circle with a yellow stencil-like design of a T-Rex inside. The lines of the piece were sloppy and jagged and surrounded by red, irritated skin.

"Yeah, that's the logo for the Red Ranger. He was my favorite when I was a kid."

"I always wanted to fuck the blue one," said Megan.

"Green Ranger was my favorite," said Ed.

"That's not the point," said Ezra taking his leg off the table. "When I first saw that I thought it was just from a black-out rager. But when I fucking found Barney this morning—which I would never get no matter how blotto I was—I knew it. I got fucking inkers."

"God damn," said Ed. "That fucking sucks. I really didn't know they were real. Just that rhyme—'don't be a fink or the inkers will ink.'"

"Yeah," said Ezra. "My parents used to sing me that before I went to sleep. I thought it was one of those stupid nursery rhymes. But it's more than that. And they even covered up my fucking Crass logo. That's how I'm *sure* it wasn't just drunk me."

"Did you know inkers were thought to be extinct?" said Megan. "DDT killed them off in the industrialized world but they were apparently still around in some pockets of the third world. With modern transportation and increased commerce, they've popped back up again."

"Why don't they just spray Ezra's building with DDT?" asked Ed.

"Because that will give everyone in the building cancer," said Megan.

"Why do you even know all that anyway?" said Ed.

"VICE had a good article," said Megan.

"That doesn't really help me right now," said Ezra.

"Dude, try not to worry too much about it," said Ed. He slapped Ezra on the shoulder. "Shit could be worse."

Ezra winced and rubbed the swollen dinosaur tattoo.

Ezra unlocked the door to his apartment building and staggered inside. The heavy door swung shut and the lock clicked behind him.

He swayed and looked up the stairs that lead to the apartments.

He was drunk but he wished he was drunker.

With each step, he was careful not to touch the walls. He studied the old carpet and the peeling wallpaper, looking for any sign of an inker.

He reached the top of the stairs. They looped around and led up to the third floor but his room was on the second.

Ezra walked down the hallway. As he passed each door he imagined the occupants asleep in their beds while tiny men with tiny tattoo guns crawled over them in the dark, scrawling tramp-stamps and barbed-wire wrist bands.

He reached his door and fumbled with his keys. Unlocking it, he inhaled deeply, opened it and flicked on the overhead light.

The bright incandescent light flooded the room and Ezra's eyes darted around trying to catch an inker scurrying for a hiding place.

But there was nothing.

Ezra shut the door but he moved no further into the room. He carefully scanned the tiny studio. The room was small but it had everything he needed – a small fridge, a microwave, a sink, a closet, his bookshelves, and a TV with an Xbox. His walls were plastered with show flyers and fold-out posters from anarcho-punk LPs. On the far side of the room was his bed and desk with his laptop and speakers. Above the desk was a window overlooking downtown Portland.

There was no sign of the inkers, but he *knew* they must be hiding somewhere.

He carefully placed his bag down on the large plushy chair he used when he played video games—he didn't dare place anything on the floor. The inkers could be hiding underneath his bed, fridge, or anywhere in the room. If just one stumbled into his bag, Ezra could take it with him the next time he left the apartment. That's how they spread.

He moved to the bed, grabbed the top blanket and threw it back quickly. Nothing scurried for cover. He inspected the white sheets for the inkers tell-tale sign of tattoo ink shit-stains but the sheets were clean and unblemished.

He backed away from the bed and looked around his room. He knew they were here somewhere.

Ezra pulled a PBR from his fridge and cracked it open. Getting shit-faced drunk was the only way he could get any sleep nowadays. Otherwise his brain would go crazy as he lay in bed, imagining the little monsters coming out from their hiding spots to give him shitty tattoos.

He sat down at his desk and turned on the computer. The room spun and he drank more.

———

Ezra woke to the mass-transit train outside his window, blaring its horn.

His head pounded from all the cheap beer he had chugged the night before. He coughed a few times.

He squinted at the day-light streaming through the window. He rubbed his eyes trying to wipe away the sleep.

That's when he noticed the fresh tattoo of a cartoon pony on the inside of his forearm.

———

Ezra came out of the shower. The recent tattoos on his arm and leg stung and itched like a motherfucker.

The apartment building was all one-room studios and the bathrooms and showers were in common areas that all the tenants shared.

Ezra opened the door that led to the hallway to see Benny. Benny lived on the third floor, right above him. He worked on video games. Ezra couldn't remember what they were called but they couldn't have been anything too successful for him to be living in a place like this.

"So I take it you got them too," Benny said pointing. "I don't really take you for a *My Little Pony* fan."

"Yep, the little fuckers got me."

"Check this out."

Benny held out his arm. There was a black and white oval face on his skin.

"What the Hell," said Ezra. "It looks like a smiling pineapple."

"I think it's supposed to be a Misfits skull."

"Well they fucked that one up."

"No shit."

Ezra rubbed his arm and winced.

"You OK?" asked Benny. "Yeah, they're sore. The fucking bastards are covering up my good shit. They fucked up both my Crass and Black Flag tattoos."

Ezra sat down and nervously rubbed his legs. "I keep thinking I can feel them crawling on me."

"Tell the landlord, he'll spray your room down with some poison. Have you seen any?"

"No."

"Me neither, which sucks. If we don't find were they're living they'll come back. I got my room poisoned three times already and they just keep coming back."

"God, I feel like I haven't slept in weeks. It's maddening. What are we going to do?"

"I don't know but they're infesting the entire building."

"So how do you not feel them?" asked Ed. "Their tattooing you, doesn't it hurt?"

"Nope," said Megan. "The tattoo guns they use have a numbing agent built right in. People who have inkers never feel it until it's too late."

"She's right," said Ezra. "Can't feel a fucking thing until morning and then you get this—"

He held out his arm and rolled up the shirt sleeve.

"Damn, *My Little Pony*," said Megan. "Some people would pay good money for that."

"Not me," said Ezra.

"At least you got Rainbow Dash," said Ed.

Ezra and Megan turned to stare at him.

"What did you say?" said Megan.

"What?" said Ed. "It could be worse, it could've been Derpy."

"You are not helping your case," said Ezra. "Regardless, it appears that my inkers have really shitty taste in TV shows."

"You could have a worse infestation," said Ed.

"Seriously? How? My skin is being permanently marked every time I try to sleep."

"There's Bloggers, they spy on you and then post the most embarrassing details about your life online. Rummagers, they steal your shit and sell it on eBay. I once had a bad case of Hippies. They smoked all my weed, kept me up all night with drum circles, *and* made my whole place smell like bad B.O. and patchouli."

"No, no, you don't understand," said Ezra. "These little fuckers hunt humans. They are not trying to feed off your embarrassment or your weed. They want to feed on *you*. Your blood. Remember how I said that I couldn't feel them? Their little needles have a numbing venom but you still bleed. They lap that shit up. Literally, they drink your blood. They can smell the carbon dioxide. They wait for you to be breathing it out in regular intervals and when you are still—in other words, asleep. So every time you lay down to sleep the Inkers are waiting. And when you do fall asleep, they come out and eat you and mark you."

"Dude," said Edward taking a sip of his beer. "That fucking sucks."

"So how's the rest of your life going?" said Megan trying to change the subject. "Didn't you mention earlier that you have a date tomorrow night?"

It was the furthest thing from Ezra's mind but that was right. He had a date with a girl he had met on an online dating website. Her name was Lacy and they both shared an interest in comic books and horror movies. They were supposed to have their first date tomorrow evening.

"Shit," said Ezra. "What am I going to say about the tattoos?"

"Low light is your friend," said Megan.

———

The date went well. Ezra wore his studded and patched-up jacket with a Mouthful of Ants back patch. It helped with his "bad boy" image, which the ladies always seemed to like. More importantly, it covered up his arms.

They went to the Baghdad Theater for a revival showing of *They Live* and hit the bars.

After a few drinks they were making out in a dark back corner and then after a few more they were back at her place fucking.

They passed out exhausted and sweaty from sex and booze. Lacy woke him up in the morning because she had to go to work.

"Damn, you slapped my ass good last night," she said. "I'm still a bit sore."

She turned her back to him and on her left cheek was a fresh tattoo of the *Two and a Half Men* logo.

———

"Jesus Christ, did you say anything?"

Ezra was sitting in Benny's room. He had hurried home from Lacy's place and ran into Benny in the apartment building's hallway. Benny invited him up for coffee.

"What was I going to say?" said Ezra. "I think I gave you inkers? I hope you really enjoy bad TV?"

"Yeah, probably. She should know."

"Yeah, you're right. I was just so embarrassed in the moment. I had to get out of there."

"Did she notice any of your tattoos?"

"Nah, we got really drunk and kept the lights off. What about you? How are yours doing?"

Benny shook his head and placed the coffee cup on his desk. He stood up and turned around, lifting his shirt.

"Fuck," said Ezra. "They gave you a swastika tramp stamp."

Benny lowered his shirt and sat back down.

"Seems like the little fuckers have moved on from bad punk rock tattoos to white power."

"Shitty TV shows don't seem so bad anymore. How's Squishy? Are they getting her?" Ezra nodded in the direction of Benny's morbidly obese cat that was snoring in the corner.

"She's fine. Inkers aren't into other mammals apparently. They prefer the real estate of humans."

"Have you seen any of them yet?"

"No. That's the damdest thing. I haven't seen them or even a sign of them. No ink blots. Not little piles of blood and ink shit. Nothing. I told you I reported it to the landlord and he searched the place and couldn't find anything either. Even asked me if I was sure I was getting inked here and not someplace else. He sprayed the place down anyway. Not that it did much good. Woke up this morning with the swastika."

"Same with me. Can't find a fucking sign of them. Where do you think they're coming from?"

"Not a clue."

"It fucks with my head. I can't sleep knowing that they are somewhere, watching me, waiting so they can come out and mark me again."

"It's been fucking with me too. But, I have an idea of how to find out."

Ezra checked his phone again. There was another angry text from Lacy. She had found the tattoo earlier in the day and knew right away that it was from inkers. She was pissed and making accusations about his hygiene and the company he kept. He'd call her tomorrow to apologize. He'd say he didn't know he was carrying them—which was technically true. They must have been hiding somewhere in his clothes. But he'd wait for her to cool down before he tried calling.

He looked over his clothes again. All day he'd been obsessively checking for inkers—jumping at every little itch or scratch. But still no sign of the little fuckers.

Ezra picked back up the book he had been reading—*The Haunter of the Threshold* by Edward Lee. He took another sip of coffee and tried to lose himself in the story.

In the opposite corner of the room Benny and Squishy snored.

Benny's plan was for Ezra to stay awake all night and keep watch while Benny slept and played the role of bait. The inker's venom kept their victims asleep so they wouldn't be woken. But someone else in the room would hear the tiny tattoo guns.

When the inkers started their guns over Benny, Ezra was to chase them away. They hoped the little bastards would flee to wherever it was they hid when humans were awake. Then they would know where the infestation was and figure out how to get rid of them.

Benny had taken sleeping pills and after a few drinks with Ezra and watching some *South Park*, Benny crawled into bed and was out.

Ezra made some coffee, not that he was that interested in sleeping. He waited, with his book, for the inkers to come.

BZZT BZZZZZT BZZT BZZT BZZZZZT

Ezra opened his eyes and sat up on the couch. The first rays of dawn were peeking through the window, casting the room in a low light.

BZZZZZZT BZZT BZZT

What was that strange noise he was hearing? His sleep-addled brain was trying to process to the sound in the room. Then it hit him.

The inkers.

He flipped on the overhead light and rushed to Benny's bed.

Benny was sleeping on his stomach with his right arm above his head. On his inner wrist was the outline of an iron cross with the inside shading just getting started.

Around his wrist were six tiny skinheads. They were about the size of a dime and each of them had tiny tattoo guns.

They looked up at Ezra and he could see surprise on their little faces. Then they turned away and ran down Benny's forearm.

Ezra darted forward and snatched one up in his hand. The inker stung him with its tattoo needle.

"Fuck," said Ezra, dropping the inker. The little skinhead hit the floor and dashed underneath the bed.

Ezra looked back at the bed where the other inkers had been but they were gone. He looked around the room and didn't see them.

"Hey, hey Benny," he said, shaking Benny's shoulder as he scanned the room trying to find the vermin.

"Hey man, wake up."

"Uhhhhh…"

"Wake the fuck up. The inkers were here."

That got through the drug and sleep haze. Benny sat up and rubbed his eyes.

"Fuck," he said when he noticed the new tattoo on his wrist. "Where…where'd they go?"

"I think they're under your bed," said Ezra. He was now down on his hands and knees using his cell phone as a flashlight. "But I don't see them."

Benny stood up. "They went under my bed?"

"I think so. I know one went under and the others were running there." Ezra pointed to the end of the bed which was against the corner wall of the room.

Benny pulled the sheets off his bed and shook them but no little skinheads fell out.

Then Ezra noticed the crack in the wall—just a foot above the bed and right in the corner. It was just half an inch wide and barely noticeable.

"Fuck," said Ezra as he back away.

"What?" said Benny.

Ezra pointed. "There."

"I don't see anything."

"They went into that crack. The little bastards are in the walls."

"Fuck, so that's how they're getting around the building," said Benny.

"Shit. Shit!" shouted Ezra.

"What?"

"Come down to my room with me."

They rushed down to the second floor and into Ezra's room. Ezra rushed over to his bed.

"I totally forgot," he said. "When I first moved in the walls were all cracked to shit." He tore down a Dead Kennedy's poster that was next to his bed. The wall beneath had several large cracks.

Ezra looked at the back of the piece of paper. "I forgot that I put up all these flyers and posters to cover that shit up."

He handed the flyer to Benny. Benny looked down at the back of it and saw spots of black, red, yellow, and purple.

"The motherfuckers are in the walls," said Ezra.

———

"So what are you going to do?" asked Megan.

Ezra and Benny were out drinking with Megan and Ed. Neither of them had gotten any rest since discovering the inkers were living in the walls.

"I don't know," said Benny, his eyes bloodshot. "If they are in the walls they are in the entire building."

"You could tell the landlord to fumigate the place," said Ed.

"He'd never do that," said Ezra. "He's still in denial that there are even inkers in the building."

They sat quiet, thinking over the situation. Benny scratched at his wrist. With the inkers in the walls there was going to be almost no getting rid of them. The landlord was useless and the other tenants even less so—most of them were one step away from living on the streets. Most of their neighbors were too accustomed to horrendous conditions to give a shit.

"What hunts them?" said Megan. "Do they have any predators or something they're scared of?"

"Like if spiders eat them, we let a bunch of spiders loose?" said Ezra through a stiffed yawn.

"You said it yourself, that they're awful," said Ed. "Which would you rather have? It's worth looking into."

"I think she has a point," said Benny taking out his smartphone. "I'm looking it up."

He swiped his phone a few times and read for a minute.

"Well shit," Benny said. "They have no known nature predator but there is one species that...uh...distracts them."

Ezra and Benny walked into the pet store and went straight over to where the feed animals were displayed in large aquariums.

There were crickets, ants, and meal worms. There were also tanks with tiny businessmen, hobos, juggalos, and other tiny people to be fed to snakes, frogs, spiders, and other pets.

"Can I help you?" asked a sales associate.

"Yeah, can we get..." started Ezra. He turned to Benny. "How many do you think we'll need?"

"A dozen for each of us should get us started. We can always come back for more."

Ezra turned back to the salesperson. "Can we get two dozen of your sailors?"

Ezra sat cross-legged on the floor in the center of his room. He breathed in and out in slow, deep, breaths, making sure to keep a steady rhythm. He stayed perfectly still trying to fool the inkers into thinking he was asleep.

His hands were in his lap atop a small cardboard box. Inside were the dozen tiny sailors they had purchased at the pet store.

Ezra was waiting for the inkers to come and upstairs. Benny was doing the same.

He had been sitting like that for three hours until he saw the inkers. There was some rustling coming from one of his posters and then five of them came scurrying down the wall. The tiny men rushed across the room toward Ezra.

This was the first time he had seen the inkers that had violated his flesh. They looked like normal tattooists with black clothes and ink and piercing covered bodies. One would never guess they had such terrible taste in television.

He waited until they were just two feet away and then he flipped open the lid of the box.

The sailors came tumbling out onto the floor. The tiny creatures were all dressed in identical blue jeans, white sleeve-less shirts, and white sailor caps. Their bodies were buff and they all had bushy mustaches. They looked around the room, surprised at their new surroundings, and then they saw the inkers. They scurried across the floor to the inkers.

The inkers froze, not sure what to do. The sailors stopped in front of them. One stepped forward and made a bunch of gestures with his hands. An inker stepped forward and did the same. They went back and forth in this unknown sign language for a few minutes and then both groups went running together toward Ezra's wall.

Holy shit, he thought. *I think this is going to work.*

Much Later.

Ezra unlocked the door to the apartment building and could immediately hear the sounds of laughter, fighting, clinking glasses, and singing.

He walked up the stairs, down the hall, and unlocked his door. The building sounded like a rowdy bar by the docks, but he had long grown use to it.

Stepping in to his room he was met with the twenty-third verse of "99 Bottles of Beer on the Wall." He must admit that he was still amazed by their shitty taste in songs but at least they were no longer singing "The Wheels on the Bus" or "Someone That I Use to Know." They were a perfect match for the untalented inkers.

He went to his desk and opened up his laptop.

Behind the singing he could hear the familiar buzz of tattoo guns. Since the sailors had infested the building they kept the inkers busy all day and night with constant tattoos. With so many demanding customers, the inkers didn't even bother the human inhabitants anymore.

Ezra checked his email and Facebook and yawned. He closed the computer and took off his clothes. Before he turned out the light he put in his ear plugs to drown out the singing.

The sailors were annoying but it was much better than before. He got in bed and closed his eyes. Soon he was asleep.

Somewhere deep in the walls, some lucky sailor was getting Leonard and Sheldon from *The Big Bang Theory* cosplaying as Supergirl and Wonder Woman tattooed on his back.

THE GG EFFECT

Dr. Kevin Michael Allin was at the University of Cambridge on a residency, teaching theoretical mathematics, when he made a terrible discovery. It was early December and his classes were long over for the day. When he didn't have to deal with grading papers or writing lectures, he liked to tinker around on his various theorems on the classroom chalkboards. He found working out his long and complex equations on a chalkboard to be more mentally stimulating than a cramped notebook.

He stepped back from the board and stared at the numbers and symbols in horror. He mentally retraced the process trying to find a mistake—there had to be a mistake.

But, no. He went over it three more times but there was not denying it. His math was correct.

Kevin sat down at one of the front row desks, took off his glasses, and rubbed his shaved heard in frustration, trying to process what he had discovered. He had no idea how much time had passed when Dr. Merle Allin—Kevin's brother and research assistant—entered the room.

Merle looked at him with some concern, and then at the chalkboards.

"Are you OK?" asked Merle.

Kevin tried to answer, but it was hard. When he looked at his brother, the memories came rushing back. Memories of how far they had come from their parents' modest house in New Hampshire. All the wonderful machines they had invented. How hard they had worked to get here, running the world's foremost study in the abstract and theoretical sciences.

"Kevin," Merle said with growing concern. "Are you alright?"

"Yeah, yeah," said Kevin shaking his head, trying to clear the disturbing and unnerving thoughts clouding his brain.

"What's the matter?" asked Merle.

Kevin stood and waved at the chalkboards. "This."

"Is that your GG Formula?" asked Merle, stroking his bushy mustache and looking it over.

"Yes."

"Come on, Kevin. You know no one else can make sense of it."

The GG Formula was something Kevin had come up with when he was in graduate school for his first masters. It stood for "General Guideline Formula." It was a masterpiece that earned him his first Nobel Prize. Kevin had figured out how to equate historical, political, and technological events into a numerical formula. This allowed him to anticipate the trends and demands of society. He could address needs before anyone knew anything was needed, and he could create new inventions before anyone else knew the direction the tech world was headed. He wrote a book about the formula—*A Simple Guide to Understanding Everything*—but no one could seem to get it to work.

It was groundbreaking. The things he created changed the course of all humanity. And he was never wrong.

"So what is it?" asked Merle. "You know, I really hate it when you pull this genius shit."

"It ends," said Kevin.

"What do you mean?"

"It just...ends."

"So you came to the end of the formula?"

"No. I came to the end of everything."

Merle looked over the hastily scratched chalk figures, but it was a meaningless gesture of trying to understand.

"To the end of everything?" said Merle. "Well that sounds just a tad bit overly dramatic. Maybe you just finally came to the end of your equation."

"No, it can't work like that. The formula should go on for as long as events happen. For it to just—stop—it means nothing will continue to happen. It can only mean the end of all things. And all the variables point to just that happening—and we're already too late to do anything about it."

Merle cocked his eyebrow at his brother.

"Something's very, very wrong," said Kevin.

"OK, you sound like you've been working way too hard and long," said Merle, motioning to the door. "You got a long day tomorrow and you need to get some rest."

"No, no," said Kevin. "I *need* to stay here and keep working on this. There must be some way to change the outcome."

"Come on, you can worry about that when we get back," said Merle. "You don't want to upset Tracy, do you?"

Kevin glanced over at mention of his wife's name. She was probably already upset. He'd barely been home that week and he still needed to pack for the three days they'd be spending in Sweden.

"OK...OK," Kevin submitted weakly.

Merle led him out of the classroom and flicked the light off.

"Just think," Merle said. "Maybe you're wrong."

The words hung in the air, thick with trepidation.

———

Kevin sat at the head banquet table in Stockholm, Sweden. The crowd was large and boisterous. Everyone was eating and drinking, celebrating his success. But Kevin felt no joy for his accomplishments. His chest had been tight with dread since his discovery.

That weekend he had just received his fourth Nobel Prize, something no other human being had ever accomplished. He should have been celebrating his success, but he just couldn't shake the feeling of an impending disaster. He could tell that Tracy had noticed that something was off, but she hadn't said anything to him—most likely just chalking it up to his award-nerves.

He cut off a piece of pheasant and slowly chewed on the greasy game bird while looking around. Tracy looked beautiful—decked out in Dolce and Gabbana for the prestigious event. Next to her were their two daughters, Nico and Ann, his eleven-year-old twins. Their lives were just starting, but they were already smart and outgoing. Beyond Kevin's numerous prizes, they were the source of his endless pride.

And then he wondered what would happen to them when it all ended and, whatever it would be, happened? Would it be quick? Would they be happy and laughing one moment and then, with no notice or sensation, be gone? Or would it be agonizing? Would they suffer…?

"Dr. Allin, a moment of your time, if you please."

Kevin turned to see an older man with no hair on his head but for a snow-white busy mustached. He held out his hand with a large smile.

Kevin shook it. "How do you do?"

The man congratulated Kevin on his unrivaled accomplishments. He said he represented a group of men—very rich men. They would fund Kevin for whatever he wanted. He would be free to pursue any flight of intellectual fantasy he wished. All they wanted was a cut of the profit from whatever he created. The man explained, that would only be fair—as they would be giving him an unlimited budget with no time constraints.

"I'll think about it," said Kevin.

"That's all I ask for," said the man as he handed Kevin a card. "Take some time to enjoy yourself and consider the possibilities. After you're home and rested, give us a call."

The man stood up to leave, but paused as if something was on his mind. He turned back to Kevin.

"I believe we can do good things together, Dr. Allin," said the man with a jovial grin. "Big things," he said, and then was gone.

———————

In the weeks after arriving home from the ceremony, Kevin could barely go through the motions of teaching his classes. His mind was constantly eager to return to studying his formula—which he did with every available moment. He barely ate and rarely slept; he was only dedicated to finding some sort of loophole or error.

But he found neither.

Once he had resigned himself that there was nothing he could do, he called the number on the card the man gave him. A quick chat and a very generous advance to his bank account proved that the stranger was not lying.

He told his wife about the new job and lied that the stress he had been under was from trying to decide on the position. It would involve a move back to the United States—New Mexico to be precise. At first Tracy and his daughters had objected, but when the financial matters—and glories—came up, Kevin was able to win them over.

He managed to work out that Merle would continue on as his assistant. So, they waited for the semester to end and then traveled back to their country of birth.

They had a large warehouse with a full staff for their studies. Kevin told them that they were working on creating the first stable transporter that could be used to instantly move large amounts of goods across the globe and, eventually, people.

But Kevin had only told Merle what they were really working on. A few years back a research team had created a large hadron collider for testing particle and high-energy physics. While it was under construction, some in the press put forward the statistically unfounded theory that the machine could create a black hole on Earth and destroy everyone. Of course, that was a silly worry. The machine was designed in no such way and unlikely to suffer such catastrophic failure.

But Kevin and Merle's machine was designed to do exactly that.

Kevin could find no way out of the ending the GG Formula predicted—they were already too far into the events that set everything in motion. The only chance for all of humanity, perhaps all of reality, was for Kevin to go *outside* of reality. From there, maybe, if he was lucky, he could alter whatever set them down this dead-end path.

The machine was designed in such a way that a subject could stand in the exact spot where a black hole would form. It would completely envelope the subject at once and, in theory, expel them outside of our fourth dimensional space—outside of the constrictions of time. From there, Kevin could travel through time to right whatever was wrong.

At least, that was their idea.

Even though Merle knew what they were really working on, there was still one secret Kevin had hidden from him.

They had been up late one night, drinking in the lab, reminiscing, when Merle asked a question.

"So, when you go through that thing, what happens to the rest of us?"

"What do you mean?"

"I mean, we're creating a black hole in a lab—which is a stupid enough idea on its own. That you're going to travel through to save humanity's future—which is even fucking stupider." Merle slurred that last part a bit. "So while you're through, what about everyone here? Will the hole suck us all in?"

"No, no," said Kevin. "It should only exist for the smallest fraction of an instant. One moment I'll be there and then I'll be gone—outside everything we know. Hopefully, I can fix it. And hopefully, I'll be back."

"And how do you think you're going to do that?"

"I'll figure it out."

Merle grunted and threw back another shot of whiskey.

Kevin stared down at his shot-glass and the amber liquid within. What he had just said was all a lie. Anything could happen when they create that black hole. It could be extremely unstable and disappear instantly, taking him with it. But it was also just as likely to rapidly expand and suck the very Earth into it.

But the world was going to end anyway and there was nothing they could do about it. Isn't it better to risk everything for one chance to save everyone? Kevin thought of his daughters. This was his only chance, slim as it may be, to give them a future.

And there was no coming back—this was a suicide mission.

He took the shot and slammed the glass down.

There was nothing to worry about. He was never wrong.

It didn't take them nearly as long as Kevin thought to finish the machine. Part of him wished it had taken longer. He had actually been working only a normal eight-hour day and then spending the rest of his time with Tracy and the kids every night—trying to enjoy what little he still had with them.

But the end of the GG Formula could happen at any moment, and he was lucky to beat its arrival.

The day it was to be turned on, Kevin and Merle sent the rest of the staff home for the afternoon. They didn't want anyone realizing what they had been constructing and shutting down the powering on process.

Kevin and Merle barely said anything to each other, both committed to the project and lost in their own thoughts of the implication.

Even while they did the final practice run, they were nothing but business.

When it was all set and ready to go, Kevin headed to his platform and Merle headed to the main control panel. Their paths crossed and they both stopped to look each other in the eyes. And then they hugged.

"Good luck, brother," said Merle.

"To you as well...brother," said Kevin.

And then they got in place.

"Ready?" asked Merle over the intercom. The main controls were in a small room that overlooked the machine. The room was shielded to protect the machine's operator from any radiation.

"Ready," confirmed Kevin.

Kevin could hear the flick of the on-switch. The machine hummed to life around him. It was a loop of garbage-can-thick metal tubes that ran in an oval the size of an Olympic track field. Leading from the main tubes were much smaller ones that ran into and through the walls surrounding him. On the other side of those walls were massive computer banks that would be performing all the complex equations and operations needed for their hacking of reality.

"Ignition in 5..." said Merle's voice over the intercom. There was a slight shake to those words.

Kevin's fists gripped tighter.

"4."

The over-head florescent lights glowed brighter.

"3."

The machine's tubes began to shake as they came to life with a loud, whirling whine.

"2."

The lights grew brighter and brighter. One exploded and rained down shards of glass.

"1."

The machine shook harder and harder and whirled louder and louder.

"Igniting."

Kevin thought of his family.

More of the lights overloaded from the massive surge of energy coursing through the building. The machine rattled to the point that Kevin briefly wondered if it was going to shake itself apart.

Then there was a noise. It was overwhelming and shattered all his senses for its millisecond duration. In that moment, he heard every man, woman, child, dog, cat, cow, fish, bird, fly, beetle, bee, flower, tree, blade of grass, and all the rest of God's creations cry out at once.

But then they all went silent.

Kevin had felt nothing, but he was definitely somewhere else. He was surrounded by complete and total blackness. Not darkness, as he could see his own body with no difficulty, but just open blackness in every direction as far as he could see.

He stepped forward and his shoe landed with a loud clunk. He looked down to see that there was a floor like pure, polished obsidian that seemed to go on forever.

He took a few more steps forward and looked around. It was almost like being in an eternal sensory deprivation chamber.

Then he saw the light. It was just a tiny pinprick of pure white, but it stood bright out against the never-ending black. And the light began to get bigger. It grew to the size of a baseball, and then a car, and then a house, and then the entire horizon.

Soon it filled his vision. The brightness hurt his eyes, and some tiny back corner of his brain felt it was being stabbed.

And then the light overtook him.

There was scenery speeding past him left and right. It was like he was on an invisible super-sonic train running under an eternal night. Only his surroundings were moving.

He walked to within a foot of objects flashing past and peered into them. There were flashes of color and depth. At times Kevin thought he saw brief glimpses of figurers—people—moving within the blur.

He moved back and waited for what he thought were just a few minutes—but there was really no way to be sure. The objects didn't show any sign of stopping.

He looked around, but nothing was changing and he didn't see anything new, just everything continuing to speed past. He looked back at the things hurtling by and considered his options.

He reached out until his fingers were just inches away.

He breathed in deep and then pushed his arm forward.

There was a bright flash and then he was in the living room of his parents' house. Above the fireplace was his grandfather's cuckoo clock with the front corner chipped away. There was the faded brown couch. And his father's recliner with a coffee table next to it with the newspaper and ashtray.

His parents both died in a car accident when he was twenty-three and away studying. He hadn't been able to come home for the funeral due to tests. The house was sold shortly thereafter. Kevin hadn't seen the room since he closed the deal with the realtor and, quite frankly, hadn't thought about the house in the many years since.

Three figures shimmered into place. His father was sitting in his chair with a content smile and a whiskey. His mother came into place on the couch. She was leaning forward with pursed lips as if she was in the middle of saying something.

The third figure appeared next to her on the couch. It was a much younger Kevin—around eight or nine. He had his head in a comic book—*Tales to Astonish*.

All three figures were perfectly still and didn't breathe or blink.

His plan had apparently worked to some degree. He was out of time in, currently, some preserved moment of his own past.

He came to the fireplace mantel, where the old wooden clock hung. The mantle was decorated with various family mementoes from his parents' past. There was a framed picture of his mother's parents, a porcelain elephant, and various other knick-knacks. He picked up a framed picture of Merle and him—they couldn't have been more than four. They were sitting outside in the grass on a bright sunny day. They both had big, joyous smiles.

Kevin set the picture down and it clinked on the hard wooden mantel.

He turned around and all three frozen people now had their heads turned. They were staring at him. They didn't appear to have moved in any other way, but all three now had quizzical expressions and were looking at his exact spot.

Kevin slowly moved to the side and they didn't move or change.

Then Kevin realized they hadn't been looking at him. They had somehow heard him setting the picture down. This gave light to a new discovery—he could interact with what he saw and experienced here.

There was a flash again, and then he was in his old bedroom. Kevin saw younger him, but older this time. Sixteen for sure. As soon as his senses took hold, Kevin remembered this specific day.

He was sitting on his bed reading a book he had checked out from the library, *The Origin of the Species* by Charles Darwin. If he could pinpoint one moment that sent him down his entire path of inventing and intellectual pursuits—it would be this. That book opened up a whole new world of mental exploration for him.

Another flash and he was in the ballroom from just a few months ago, receiving his fourth Nobel Prize. Like before in these out-of-time travels, all the people were frozen in place.

Then another flash. He was standing in the ruins of some massive city. What used to be skyscrapers were now just smoldering empty husks. The streets were filled with broken concrete and twisted metal. Fires burned but the flames were still in the air, like a freeze-frame from a movie.

In front of him were two human corpses. Their clothing and skin had been completely burned away, leaving them red and black like overdone barbecue.

This was the end he predicted. The end of everything. But how did things get so bad, so fast? What could he possibly do to prevent it?

And then it hit him. He wasn't seeing an overview of his past. He was seeing the events that led to this. Somehow, he was the one responsible for the end of the world. All this death and destruction—it was because of him.

It was his influence on the world that led to this end. His GG Formula wasn't just accurately predicting what was coming next—he had been solving for the end.

It was all his fault.

Guilt and depression hit him, hard. His legs gave way and he fell to the ground. In his attempts to improve all of mankind, he had ruined it. He took everyone's future away. His family...

But then a new resolve hit. This is what he was here to prevent. He had a rare opportunity. This was no mere premonition of what was to come. He could still fix it.

There was a flash and he was in his old hometown library. He saw himself at the counter with a small stack of books. The frozen old librarian smiled at his sixteen year-old-self.

Kevin went over and looked through the books his younger-self was checking out. There, in the middle, was *The Origin of the Species*.

He stuck *The Origin of the Species* on a shelf and grabbed another book at random. He looked down at it, *The War of the Worlds* by H.G. Wells. A fun little potboiler that he read later in his life. It was enjoyable, but these flights of fancy were never really his thing.

Kevin replaced *The War of the Worlds* in the middle of the stack. Without *The Origin of the Species*, he never would have had that inspiration, at that key point in his life, to pursue the sciences.

Now it was just a matter of where his life would go.

There was a flash and he found himself in another ballroom—not the same one from his Nobel receptions, but still ornately decorated and filled with people in fine suits and expensive dresses.

An older version of him was at the front table as he was receiving a Pulitzer Prize. He must have grown into a writer in this new timeline.

Kevin smirked. *Well, at least I'll still be good at something.*

A flash and he was back to standing in the ruined city. Nothing had changed.

What? he thought with indignation. He had changed the past, but yet he was still seeing a doomed future. This couldn't be right!

So he went back again. He changed it so he grew into a painter, a baseball player, and even a star ballerina. In each scenario, he saw himself becoming recognized for his achievements and then the same image of burning buildings and dead people.

No matter what he changed, his influence still damned everyone and everything.

Was there nothing he could do to change the future? Was this a futile mission?

He flashed back to his parents' living room when he was much younger. The first place he went to when he entered this strange plane of existence.

Kevin smiled sweetly at his mother and father. They had loved him so much and were so kind and caring. Little did they know that their little boy would grow up to be the cause of the apocalypse.

Then, he knew why this was the first stop on his journey. It wasn't the book that set him out on his course in life—it was this that prepared him so well for the future. His parents had raised him with support and guidance. He was so well equipped for whatever path he chose that he could *only* succeed.

That's what he had to change.

A flash and he saw a very young boy, no more than three, sitting on the floor of a log cabin. He knew this was his father. It was so strange to look at someone who helped create you, so young and so fragile. His father, as a baby, had an expression of pure joy and happiness. He was playing with a toy train on the floor.

Kevin picked up the toy.

It felt wrong. He didn't like taking a toy from a child, much less one that would one day later be so loving to him.

But the knowledge of what he had to do gnawed at his consciousness. While this would feel bad in the moment, it was for the good of everyone to come.

He threw the toy as hard as he could at a nearby window and, to his surprise, the glass shattered with a loud crash. It was the first noise and movement from something other than himself since he came here.

There was a flash and Kevin was still in the same room. His father, still as a baby, was sitting on the floor—mid-scream with tears frozen across his face. A man and woman stood over him. It must have been Kevin's grandparents, with stern looks on their faces, scolding the child.

Kevin traveled through his father's life. Changing as much as he could in little ways. Changing his tests from school to give him failing grades, destroying his paychecks, moving his possessions around to subtly shatter what he thought he knew of object permanence.

At this, he felt guilt. His actions were having cruel effects. Kevin did everything he could to make his father's life much more difficult in little ways. He knew from the way his father had told Kevin of his past that he prided himself on always being a hard worker and that the world had rewarded him for his toils with a beautiful home and family.

But now Kevin was changing his father's past so that every step of his life would be just a desperate attempt at survival. With no prospects for the future and a never-ending string of "bad luck," he would not be the same man who raised Kevin.

But then the guilt left and Kevin was resigned to his mission. This was bigger than him or his father.

And Kevin was back in the room with his much younger self. But everything was different. His younger self was sitting on the floor, mid-cry. He was not in the house he remembered from his youth, but in a log cabin just like the one he saw from his father's past. The place was dirty and in a state of disarray with crushed beer cans and cigarette butts littering the floor.

The biggest change was his father sitting in a chair in the corner. He no longer looked like the middle-class happy family man Kevin remembered. In his place was a man wearing stained and torn clothes. His hair was grown past his shoulders and frayed. His face was unshaved with days old patchy spots.

It was in his eyes that there was the biggest difference. These were not the soft and understanding eyes Kevin remembered. These were wild, like a caged animal longing for something weaker to let its guard down and venture too close. There was cruelty and insanity sparking.

Kevin shivered.

A flash and Kevin saw his sixteen-year-old self. He was not in his room reading, like he remembered doing most of that part of his youth. He was now on a street corner in what was obviously a very bad part of the city. His younger self was dressed in little more than rags and giving a baggie of something green to another kid on the corner.

Kevin moved closer and saw that he was giving marijuana to the other kid.

Great, I became a drug dealer.

Then another flash and Kevin saw himself as a young man. He knew it was him but there was little physically in common with what he viewed as himself. He was on stage at some dingy club singing in front of a band. He was dressed only in a jockstrap. His head was shaved and he had a mangy goatee. Blood was splattered over his body from open wounds on his chest and forehead.

The band backing him looked like the type of people Kevin would normally dismiss as "scum." Then he noticed Merle. He was playing a bass guitar and, just like Kevin, looked like a ruined shadow of his former self.

Oh Merle, I doomed us both.

A flash and he was in a cemetery. He was behind a tombstone that some degenerate wearing a patched-up and metal-studded leather jacket was pissing on.

Kevin didn't need to look at the monument. He knew this was his new future. To be honored by some punk pissing on his eternal resting spot.

A flash and he was in some city from out of his wildest dreams. There were people everywhere wearing strange fashions that reminded him of those cheesy sci-fi B-movies of his youth. Above him, frozen in the air, were machines that invoked cars but had no wheels and were mid-flight.

The future, he thought. It worked. This time everything didn't end.

He just needed to remove himself from the equation and everything would work out OK for everyone. Humanity would still have a future, as long as he didn't contribute to it.

And with that, he was done. He knew deep inside, in some primal corner of his mind, that he accomplished what he had set out to do. Humanity would continue on now that he wasn't here to fuck it all up.

He wondered what was next. Would he feel anything? Would there be any sort of awareness after? After this incredible journey, would there be any more adventures?

With nothing else to do, Kevin reset reality with his mind and time resumed.

And then there was nothing at all—he was gone.

June 27, 1993. The Gas Station, Manhattan.

GG Allin sat in the bathroom of the small, dank, dirty club. The air was hot that night and the venue smelled like a mix of wet dog and gasoline. He was alone, but could hear the opening band through the rotten walls. His head swirled as the mish-mash of chemicals did their thing.

Some no-name shitty band was just finishing their set and soon it would be time for him to go on. He'd been at a friend's house, which was practically next door, doing coke. He didn't want to deal with any of the opening bands or the poor, fucked-up souls who would bother to show up to something like this.

There was the instrument drone of the band finishing their last song and some half-hearted applause that quickly diminished to conversation.

He sat on the dirty toilet seat with his eyes closed. He had to psych himself up. He had to be ready to rage.

Bang—Bang—Bang

"Yo," said a voice from the other side of the bathroom door. "You ready? It's time."

"OK," said GG Allin.

He went out to perform and give it his all. He didn't know it would his last show.

Later that night, GG Allin would go to a party and die, drugged and depressed. His corpse would sit with no one knowing that he had passed on. Partygoers would pose with his body for pictures—thinking that he was just doing the junkie nod instead of a full respiratory failure. It would be several hours before anyone would think to check if he was OK.

GG Allin died and all was right with the world.

THE DOG WHO STARED

"BRUTUS IS STILL OUT THERE. He won't come in. I shook his food bowl but the little guy paid no mind."

Arthur stood up and walked across the kitchen to join his wife, Dorothy. They both looked out the window over the sink to their dog, Brutus in the back yard.

Brutus was a west highland terrier. A small white dog with pointed ears that weighed, while wet, fifteen pounds. He was what you would call an "ankle biter."

He was sitting in the center of the backyard staring straight up into the sky.

"What do you think he's looking at?" asked Arthur.

"I don't know."

Arthur went out the back door into the yard. They lived in the woods, so the yard was just a large grass clearing surrounded by trees.

Arthur clapped his hands, "Brut. Hey, Brute."

The dog ignored him.

He clapped and called again but the dog paid no attention. He walked over to Brutus and stood next to the dog, looking down. Brutus just stared up into the sky past Arthur.

Arthur turned and looked up. Where the dog was looking there was nothing but clear blue sky. He wasn't looking at some squirrel high up in a tree.

"Hey, come on," Arthur patted the dog on the head. "It's time for dinner."

Brutus still ignored him.

Arthur shrugged and went back inside.

"He wants to stay out, I guess," Arthur said to Dorothy. "He's got a dog door. He'll come in when he's hungry."

———————

"He's still out there," said Dorothy.

Arthur and Dorothy were standing at the kitchen window the next morning. They were both in robes, holding their cups of coffee.

Brutus had been outside all night instead of his normal place at the foot of their bed. He was still in the same spot outside, sitting and staring.

"What is he doing . . ." Dorothy wondered out loud.

"I don't know," said Arthur. "But I have to get ready for work."

———————

"What's with your dog?"

"Huh?" Arthur looked up from the engine. It was Friday and Arthur's buddy, Brad, had come over to take a look at the latest improvements to Arthur's 1950 Chevy Club Coupe. The two were going to take it out for a drive later.

"He's just been sitting there . . . staring," said Brad.

"Yeah, he's been doing that lately."

"Why do you think? It's kinda . . . weird."

"He's a dog. Here, take a look at this."

Brad didn't respond. Arthur looked over and saw his friend staring at Brutus.

"Hey," Arthur shouted. "Can you take a look at this."

Brad shook his head like he was coming out of a daze. "Yeah. Sure. Sorry."

"I didn't know your friends were coming over today."

"What?"

Dorothy motioned towards their backyard. "Brad, John, Frank, and Stan are out back. They've been here for at least an hour."

"Really?" asked Arthur. He had made no plans with them.

He went out into the backyard. His friends were sitting in lawn-chairs around Brutus, who was still staring into the sky. They had brought a giant cooler, and they were sipping their beers while silently watching the dog.

"Ummm . . . hey guys," said Arthur. "What's up?"

Brad looked at him but the rest of his friends paid no attention.

"Hey man," said Brad. "I just told the guys about Brutus and they all wanted to come over and take a look."

Arthur looked them over and asked, "why?"

Brad shrugged. "Dunno. Seemed interesting."

When Arthur and Dorothy got back from work the next day there were two dozen people in their backyard. Some they recognized—there was Gary from the post office and some teen girl from the grocery store. There were a few people they didn't know at all. The crowd was all sitting in lawn on folding chairs they brought or were standing. Everyone was facing Brutus.

Arthur pushed through the crowd to Brad, who was still sitting in his chair in the front row.

"What the Hell is going on?" demanded Arthur.

"Some people wanted to have a look." Brad replied, never looking up from Brutus.

Arthur, frustrated, made his way back to Dorothy.

"What do they want?" she asked.

"They just want to have a look."

"Well . . . as long they're being quiet."

Arthur and Dorothy went inside and watched TV.

"How many people do you think are out there?" asked Dorothy.

Arthur shook his head. "At least a hundred is my guess."

Dorothy pointed. "They have a hot-dog stand."

Over the past few days, more and more people had been showing up in their backyard. They all joined those already gathered, watching Brutus.

Brutus, who was normally a very excitable and friendly dog, paid no attention to the people. Arthur and Dorothy had been growing concerned with how long he'd been outside, seemingly without food or water—both his bowls remained untouched since the day he started staring. But he seemed no worse for wear and still ignored their calls.

"I've had enough, let's get going," said Arthur.

Arthur and Dorothy had gotten tired of the craziness that was now their backyard. They had decided on a weekend camping getaway. Their bags were packed and in the car.

They could deal with this stupidity later.

The trip had been great and they had almost forgotten what was going on in their backyard until he turned onto their street.

The street ended only a few hundred yards after the turn-off to their home and it began only a half-mile before. In total, there were only seven homes on the road. Normally it was very quiet and they rarely saw their neighbors.

But today, there were scores of cars and hordes of people. Rides, carnival games, and food carts were set-up.

Arthur pulled over and parked the car next to a Ferris wheel.

"What is this all about?" asked Dorothy as they got out of the car.

"I have no . . . oh, God . . ." Arthur lost the sentence when he saw the T-shirt vendor. A line of people waited to buy screen printed shirts with the image of two intense staring eyes and the slogan: I KNOW WHAT THE DOG SEES!

It was impossible. There was no way all these people were here because of their dog—because of Brutus. But as Arthur and Dorothy made their way through the mass and got closer to their house, the crowd grew thicker and all attention was directed towards their house.

There was no denying it. All these people were here because of Brutus.

When they got to their backyard people were taking pictures of Brutus, cheering him on, and waving signs that read: STARE, DOG, STARE. NEVER GIVE UP. I BELIEVE IN THE DOG.

Arthur stumbled out of the people, finally finding himself in open space. He turned around to see his dog, still in the same position staring, and his four friends, still sitting in lawn chairs, sipping beer, and watching Brutus.

"Hey man, nice to see you again," said Brad raising a beer.

"What is going on? Where did all these people come from?" shouted Arthur, struggling to be heard over so many people.

Brad shrugged. "Dunno. Guess they wanted to see your dog."

A man can only take so much before he finally breaks and this was Arthur's breaking moment. He moved in front of Brutus and turned to the crowd, waving his arms in the air. "You people are insane! Why are you here? It's just a fucking stupid dog for God sake!"

The crowd immediately went silent and for one brief wonderful moment, Arthur thought he had gotten through to them. But he quickly realized that everyone around was not paying attention to him but Brutus. He looked down at the dog and saw that he had moved aside. He was no longer sitting and staring but hoping around and wagging his little white tale.

The crowd was watching Brutus with fascination and then turned as one to look up the sky behind Arthur, the exact same place Brutus had been staring.

Arthur slowly turned around and looked up. The sky was a clear pristine blue with not a cloud to be seen. But there was a fiery ball hurtling straight towards him.

He had no chance to register the oncoming object. The soccer ball sized meteor hit him in the chest and tore straight through his body, splattering blood and organs onto Brad and his three other friends.

The meteor hit the ground and bounced over Brad. The crowd parted for the extraterrestrial object in hushed reverence. The meteor bounced two more times and Brutus tore off after it. Bouncing along and barking and throwing his paws into the air, Brutus had finally gotten his new toy.

THE MOST ACCOMPLISHED
CRACKHEAD IN THE WORLD

BRIAN HAD A GREAT LIFE. He married his high school sweetheart, Mary, at twenty-two. They had three wonderful kids, Katy, Michele, and David. They were all on the honor-roll and varsity sports teams. They never ceased to make Brian and Mary proud. Brian had a career at the Internal Revenue Service. Numbers and order were his passion. And everything in his life was in place and perfect.

That's why he started doing crack.

You must understand that Brian was not ungrateful or going through some sort of mid-life crisis. He was perfectly content and happy with everything he had. He was just bored. Life held no challenge, excitement or surprise.

He wasn't even completely sure what made him want to try crack. One day at the office the idea just popped into his head and he couldn't get it out. It seemed just like the spice that he needed.

Brian had never bought illegal drugs before, but it turned out to be surprisingly easy. When he got off work he went to Old Town, a part of downtown, home to numerous Chinese restaurants, strip clubs, and dive bars. He knew from watching THE WIRE that drug dealers normally wore baggy coats to hide their stash.

After a few minutes of walking around he spotted a young man wearing just that sort of coat milling about a corner. Brian walked up to him and smiled.

"Excuse me young man, I'd like to buy some crack. Are you..." what was that phrase from TV? Oh, yeah, "holding? Or do you know anyone who is?"

The gangsta's eyebrows were shaved off and in their place the words FUCK and OFF were tattooed.

He cocked FUCK up at Brian, "Yo, you po-po?"

"If you mean police, I can assure you I am not."

The youth nodded and glanced around, "Aight, I got wha yo need. Tweny."

Brian took out his wallet and gave him the money. In return he got a small matchbox-sized plastic bag half-filled with small, dusty, chalk-white rocks. He carefully placed the purchase into his front pocket, said "Thanks good sir," and hurried back to his car.

He sat in the front seat inspecting his drugs. *His drugs!* He never even so much as smoked marijuana before but here he was with crack. He took the bag out of his pocket and held it up so he could get a good look at it in the sunlight. The rocks were so small but seemed so intimidating.

He gently placed the bag back in his pocket and patted the slight bulge. He smiled, excited and just slightly nervous, and he drove away. But then one thought popped into his mind.

How do I do it?

A quick Google search in the privacy of his study answered all his questions. He took another trip out and bought a scouring pad and one of those fake roses that come in a glass tube. After consulting the walkthrough several more times, he had himself a crack pipe.

Brian loaded up the pipe and nervously looked it over. This was it. He lit up, took a hit, and sat back in his office chair. The smoke was sweet and harsh and he immediately started hacking. This was so much worse than that cigarette in tenth grade.

Instantly his brain was awash with the drug. He suddenly had so much energy. And he felt good. No, not good, fucking great! He felt like he could do anything.

He paced around the study. He had so much energy; he didn't

know what to do with himself. Mary and the kids were out at the movies and were going grocery shopping after, so he had the house to himself for a few hours.

On his desk was a quarter-finished ship in a bottle. The project and been going on and off for two years but he could never seem to find the time or inspiration to finish it.

He got out the modeling glue, sat down, took another hit of crack and got to work.

A few short hours later Mary knocked on the door and walked in this office, "Hi honey, we're back and I'm going to get started on dinner. How was your afternoon?"

Brian had just come down from his last bowl and was sitting back looking at his perfect replica of the USS Enterprise CV-6. In three hours, he had finished something he had been working on for years. Now, because of crack, it was finally done.

He looked up at his wife through blood-shot, shaky eyes. "Oh...it was good."

A few days later Brian was thinking of crack again. This scared him a little. He didn't want to become a drug addict, a crackhead of all things, but it had been so much fun and he couldn't get it off his mind. And he did finish the model...

So that Saturday, when Mary was taking the kids out again, he went back to Old Town and bought some more crack.

He rushed back to his home and went straight to his study. He smoked his crack and, just like before, his head swirled and he was full of energy—full of inspiration.

He sat down at his computer and opened up Word. It had been awhile since he wrote. He used to entertain dreams of being a Harlequin romance author. He wanted to tell scandalous bodice rippers that women would masturbate to in their lonely moments.

The words flew out and he typed out all the years' worth of steamy scenes that he had never let out.

After a few short hours, and a few more hits, the novel was finished. He twitched in his chair and grinned like the Cheshire Cat.

THE EROTIC ADVENTURES OF MISS DAISY AND HER SUPER PUSSY, FLUFFY WHISKERS was 180,000 words and, in his opinion, the greatest romance novel ever written.

After a quick spell-check, he uploaded the book for sale on Amazon Kindle.

He came down shortly thereafter and Katy and the kids came home. She made wonderful, but slightly dry and bland, pork chops for dinner. Brian scarfed them down and picked at some ingrown hairs on his forearms.

He didn't give the novel another thought.

Two months, two crack binges, and two sequels to THE EROTIC ADVENTURES OF MISS DAISY AND HER SUPER PUSSY, FLUFFY WHISKERS later, Brian awoke one day to an email from Amazon, notifying him that he received his first royalty payment for his book.

Wow, he thought, *people actually bought it?*

He went to his bank's website and logged in, curious to see how much he got.

When the screen loaded, he dropped his coffee cup.

Transfer from Amazon: 737,666.23

He promptly quit his job and his family rejoiced over their newfound fortune. Brian told them that he had been writing the novels piece by piece for years late at night when he couldn't sleep.

He bought more crack and wrote more novels. He wrote so many that his fans couldn't keep up with buying them. So, Brian began to stockpile manuscripts on his hard drive. Soon there were enough books to keep his family living cushy for years.

But now he needed a new way to pass the time on crack. He just could sit there twitching like other cocaine hydrochloride enthusiasts.

Crack greatly improved his reading speed and he studied math,

Latin, philosophy, and physics. With a break for a six-day marathon of STAR TREK: DEEP SPACE NINE.

After some meticulous trial and error, he came up with a formula to balance the national budget. He did the only sensible thing—he emailed the president.

> What up!?!1!!
>
> Attached is a formula to balance the budget—also a recipe for French dip and a 20,000 word essay on the importance of the legality of scouring pads. You can forward them onto the appropriate people.
>
> Your friend,
>
> Brian
>
> P.S. Where can I buy a fancy teleprompter?

The recipe and essay were ignored but some bored intern read the formula and punched in the numbers.

It worked!

He rushed it to his supervisors and soon the formula made it all the way to the Treasury Department. It was immediately applied and the nation's financial woes were solved.

The president even had Brian flown out to Washington where Brian, his eyes bloodshot and picking at invisible bugs under his skin, accepted the Presidential Medal of Freedom.

But it was on the plane ride home, as his fingernails bleed and his unwashed clothes stank, that he wondered *is all this crack healthy?*

When the plane touched down in Portland, Brian had decided he was going to go clean.

Mary was not stupid. She knew her husband had been on drugs for weeks. She noticed his erratic changes in behavior and sudden mood swings.

Also, while doing her weekly search of his study she found his stash.

Now you have to understand that Mary was not a bad wife. She saw how the drugs were destroying Brian's body. His lips becoming concentration-camp thin and his gums bleed constantly. She has just grown accustomed to the standard of living his novels were able to afford.

So, when Brian came back from Washington, and his skin started to clear up and he was no longer constantly ranting, she became concerned.

He wasn't writing any new books and the sales of his back catalogue were slipping. Government leaders and business tycoons were offering him obscene amounts of money for more solutions to national and global problems, but seemed like the sober Brian knew less about the political, sociological, and economic workings of the world than the cracked-out Brian.

It was after the first time she went grocery shopping and Brian said to her, "don't buy any foie gras this time. We need to cut back a bit," that she knew she needed to do something.

Brian walked through his front door and froze. His dear wife Mary and his wonderful children Katy, Michele, and David were all sitting in the living room, their faces tight with anxiety and concern.

Most puzzling was the full film crew—two cameramen, a soundman with a boom mic, and someone, Brian assumed it was the director, sitting in a folding chair, sipping a Starbucks and consulting a clipboard. Two young female interns flanked him, each with their own clipboard.

"Action," the man said.

"Honey," began Mary, "can you have a seat. We need to talk."

Brian slowly walked into the room, puzzled, and sat down in his recliner. One of the cameras buzzed as it zoomed in.

Mary coughed and cleared her throat, buying time before she began. She looked over her husband. Brian had been going out for daily walks and was eating regularly. His once gaunt body was gaining color and muscle.

It disgusted her.

Each pound he put back on was a drop in their net worth. Each pimple that disappeared was one less dinner at Le Green.

She glanced at the cameraman. This was all her idea. A quick call to the station's office and she was on the phone with the producers. They were intrigued. No one had ever wanted to do an intervention of this sort before. And they were willing to offer enough money, due to Brian's minor celebrity status, to make up for his missed work.

She faced her husband. "Brian, we love you but the choices you have been making are affecting us all."

Their children all nodded.

Brian looked at them, confused.

"When you were on the drugs, we were all so happy. You provided for your family. There was nothing we were at want for.

"And when you spent your time creating, all pock-marked and twitching, I loved you. Now—" She met his eyes and then looked down. "Kids do you have anything to say?"

They glanced at each other and Katy, being the oldest, went first.

"Jacqueline Marshall is getting a Porsche, what am I going to do?"

"Killatron 6000 comes out in two weeks with a monthly subscription fee. My current allowance can't handle it," chimed David.

"I want a pony," pouted Michele.

Brian looked from each of his children to his wife and saw their disappointment.

"I'm...I'm sorry," he said. "I had no idea."

Mary looked him deeply in the eyes. "I just want the man I love back."

Brian nodded, tears welling up. "I'll do anything."

Mary stood up and walked across the room. "Hold out your hands."

He did—palms up and cupped together.

Mary placed a glass pipe, a fat white rock already loaded up, and a lighter in them.

"Please," she said. "For us."

Brian looked to his children and his wife again. Their eyes hopeful and begging him to do the right thing.

He took a deep hit.

One could feel the love in the room as Brian exhaled the sweet-smelling smoke. Their family was back.

The director and the two interns couldn't contain themselves and they wept and applauded.

In the following weeks, life went back to the way it was before. Brian started writing again and his family was able to get whatever they wanted.

He went back to studying mathematics, business, and politics and eventually started a consultation business. He picked up clients that went all the way up to the White House and United Nations and, in just two-months, brought piece to the Middle East, democracy to North Korea, and mariachi music to South Africa.

Brian smoked crack and made his family happy and the world a better place, until he OD'ed and died of a heart attack at thirty-three.

I'VE SEEN ENOUGH HENTAI TO KNOW WHERE THIS IS GOING

[Fade in on a slutty, curvy punk chick. She is hanging in the air, bound and held in place by vines wrapped around her wrists and ankles.

She struggles and the vines pull tighter. The ragged tank-top and hot-pink booty-shorts tear in her thrashing. Her tits and ass threaten to burst free.

Her green spiked Mohawk stays standing-tall.

Cut to a downward view from above the vixen.

Producer's Note: Make sure the down-shirt view of her tits is in focus. None of that amateur shit.

The camera shifts focus and we see she is hanging above a cavernous pit. A booming roar echoes from the darkness.

Cut to a close up of the girl's chest as she struggles and screams louder. Her shirt finally tears free and her tits burst out.

Another roar and she shakes around screaming. The camera zooms in on the jiggling.

Cut to the overhead view again.

We can see movement in the darkness beneath her. A giant shape wells up. Massive tentacles unspool from the black ink. The body of the beast rises up and the giant is the size of a building. Bat-like wings jut from its back. Its head looks like an elephant but dozens of tentacles, as thick as minivans, jut from the obscene face.

Cut to the creature towering before the bound woman. She trashes even harder. It looms before her, its tentacles flick the air a few more times and then fall limp.

The girl glances down and shakes and screams even louder, making sure to puff out her chest so the camera gets a good view.

The beast raises massive claws and roars, shaking its flaccid tentacles.

The woman looks down again at the limp tentacles and her body relaxes. She stares the creature in the eyes and looks fucking annoyed and pissed.]

"Seriously?"

"Cut! Cut!" shouts Bum Biggler from his director's chair.

"Seriously!?! Are you even looking at these tits? A faggot eunuch could get it up to these tits!" she shouted at the monster.

The beast looked down, dejected.

"Can someone get me the fuck down?" she yelled.

"Veronica, Veronica, I know, I know—" boom the director through the megaphone."

"No, you don't know! Do you have any idea how wet and lubed up I need to be to take that," she nodded to the beast's tentacles but wouldn't look at them. "My pussy is ready *now*. My ass is ready *now*. My mouth is ready *now*. I need a costar that is ready *now*."

She was lowered to the ground and interns ran up to undo her straps.

She glared at the director. "And to you I'm Ms. Chaos."

Another intern ran up, a beefy young man wearing nothing but platform boots and a leather thong. He held out a mirror with three neatly cut lines of coke. Veronica leaned over and snorted one.

"If you need me I'll be in my trailer. Masturbating." She glared at the creature. "*Someone's* gotta get me off."

She stormed off the set, her sexy coke slave following closely behind.

The monster watched her go.

"Oooooo...," it moaned and the thing's tentacles dangled even limper.

He turned to the thing, "It's OK, big guy. It happens to the best of us. Why don't you go take ten and we'll send someone in to help you out?"

The beast shrugged, turned, and went stomping off. Each step boomed and made the whole set shake. Bum watched his other star walk off the set.

Once the thing was gone, he held up the megaphone and addressed the crew. "We don't need another fucking dud, where's the new guy?"

———

Life had been going pretty bad for Jacob. Truthfully, it was fucking horrible. Within the past two months, his parents died in an airplane crash, his fiancé left him for a professional mime, his IT firm was bought out by some Saudis', and he was in the first round of lay-offs, his Xbox broke, his apartment got infested with bed bugs, and his dog ran away—he assumed out of shear disgrace and disgust over how pathetic his owner had become.

The little savings he had ran out pretty quickly and, with no one to turn to for help, Jacob had to take some drastic measures.

That's how he got into porn.

Having one's orifices ravaged by strangers wasn't the career he had in mind but it kept the lights on and his belly full, even if it did leave his asshole sore and his stomach lurching.

He didn't have the most ripped abs or the tightest asshole but he did learn he could deep throat, better than any of his exes in fact, and that particular skill ensured he had plenty of work.

That's how he met Bum Biggler. The short, shady, Sicilian was impressed with Jacob's work and hired him to be the exclusive fluffer for Bum's films. It was better than the free-lance work he was doing before and he didn't have to worry about any family or friends seeing him in a movie (all his work was off camera).

And even though most of his work day was spent gagging on a cock, occasionally he got some perks. Like the time he went down on Wendy Wednesday for forty-five minutes. Or when he ass-fucked Barbra Bright while she checked her email (she wanted to stay loose).

So when Bum asked him to be the fluffer on his latest flick, THE DOOM THAT CUMMED ON VAGINATOWN, Jacob jumped at the chance. Veronica Chaos was the only listed star. Bum had warned Jacob that this would be one of his "specialty" pics. Meaning Veronica would most likely be sucking off pigs or sticking needles through her nipples but Jacob didn't care. She'd need someone to tongue off her cunt or ass in-between takes.

Sometimes this job had its perks indeed.

So Jacob sat in a waiting room reading an old issue of WIZARD MAGAZINE, his dick hard as he waited for Veronica.

At the far end of the room, the door popped open and a PA poked her head through.

"Jacob, we need you."

He stood up and followed her through the door. She was young, twenty at best, with small apple tits and long lean legs leading to a small, almost boy-like ass. Just how Bum liked them. And judging by her slight limp, he was living up to his name.

She led him down several halls and around a few corners until they were at a plain, unmarked door.

"The star needs you. Now." The PA punctuated the last word with a cunt turn and walked away.

His palms were sweaty and he was slightly nervous. He had seen all of Veronica's movies—TWO MACHETES ONE GIRL, FUCK ME LIKE A KLINGON, DOCTOR WHO'S IN MY ASS—all of them.

She wouldn't care about him. He knew that he would be just another face buried between her thighs, just to keep her wet enough for the next horse cock or baseball bat. But it was good enough for him.

The room was a giant dark cavern. Slime coated the floors, walls, and ceilings. Jacob could taste it in the air—it reminded him of that old Ecto Plasma Kool-Aid. Everything seemed to be made of rock and there was no light but for some strange earthly glow coming from above, as if the room held its own dying sun.

It took Jacob a moment for his eyes to adjust and then he saw his client.

The thing was like a mountain in the room. Jacob thought it was some kind of strange set decoration but then it shifted and subtly rose and fell as it breathed. The thing was alive.

Was he supposed to service *this*?

The mass shifted toward him and he could see massive tentacles in the hazy light. He immediately knew what was expected for him and imaged them against his ass and or probing his mouth.

Sure, Jacob had blown a donkey or two in his day but this was too much.

He rushed to the door and gripped the knob. Just as he was about to throw open the door and flee, a great low moan, like a whale song, came from the colossus.

He turned back and saw the tentacles from the monster lying limp. They had no desire to violate him and this made him pause. Since he got involved in this business he had never ran into anything that didn't want to go up his ass.

"Oooooooo…" moaned the monster.

The beast looked and sounded sad. And, for some reason deep inside that Jacob would never truly understand, Jacob felt pity. He walked away from the door and back toward the thing.

"What's…what's wrong?" he asked as he inched closer to the creature.

His eyes had adjusted to the gloom and he could now make out what the monster looked like. It was a massive beast with an elephant-like head but instead of a trunk, numerous look octopus-like tentacles jutted forth. From its back were two colossal bat-like wings.

"Ooooooo…" it moaned again. Its shoulders slumped and the tentacles and wings hung slack.

There was a pathetic quality to the creature that spoke to Jacob. In the sadness of the thing's dinner dish sized eyes, he felt pity.

He approached the monster. Its tentacles were lying across the floor like power cables.

Jacob stroked one of the tentacles. "There. There. It's…OK."

The creature's sad eyes looked at him and then rolled away.

"Dude, don't be like that. We've all been there. Sometimes things just…don't work."

The creature sighed again, its huge bulk heaving. Jacob could tell he wasn't helping.

"There's a lot of pressure put on us. People think it's easy, why couldn't you get it up with the hotties we work with?"

The thing's eyes turned.

"But it's work. And work gets boring. Doesn't matter if you're filling pot-holes, spread-sheets, or pussy."

They both sighed.

Jacob sat down and patted the closest tentacles. "But man, fuck it, beats a real job. Let me ask you this, would you rather be fuckin' that bitch out there or would you want to be stuck in some bullshit cubicle?"

The thing lifted its head.

"Really, this is survival," finished Jacob with his head down.

The tentacles began to twitch and Jacob stood. The thick green fleshy cables whipped around in the air.

"Glad…glad I could be of help. You go get her."

The thing made no motion to leave but instead wrapped three tentacles around Jacob. They held him tight while their tips softy caressed his back and legs.

"Ummm… yo, what's—"

A fourth tentacle slipped between his legs and Jacob's words were lost. He gasped and got hard.

The thing's touch was firm but caring, and most importantly, felt fucking good. The tip of its tentacle wrapped around Jacob's tip.

The beast's eyes met Jacob's and the thing cooed. The pleasant purring made Jacob's body vibrate and hum.

With one suave motion, one of the tentacles pulled down his pants and turned him around. Another tentacle was there for him to be bent over.

"Ohhh..." said Jacob and yet another tentacle probed at his asshole—just teasing.

This wasn't the kind of work he had hoped for but for the first time in a long time he felt truly willing, wanting.

He closed his eyes and relaxed.

BAM!

The door to the cavern slammed open. Bum Biggler stood there and looked at Jacob with his puckered asshole out and ready.

"Great job," shouted Bum. "But he needs to save it for the shoot."

Jacob looked back and saw that the monster's tentacles were now whipping through the air.

He stood and pulled up his pants.

"Alright, take five, man," said Bum as Jacob walked past. He turned to the monster, "you, on set in two. We don't want to miss..." he gestured at the flicking tentacles, "this."

But before Jacob passed through the door he turned back at the beast. It was looking at him too. Their eyes locked.

And they both felt a pang somewhere inside.

———

Jacob stood to the side of the set. Watching scenes get filmed was another perk he occasionally got to enjoy.

The monster was really letting Veronica Chaos have it. There was one tentacle in her mouth, pussy, and ass, with three wrapped around her waist, and yet another two choking her.

The beast pumped and Jacob watched. The thing kept his attention on thrusting and fucking and abusing Veronica but, at one brief moment, its attention was diverted. Its eyes flashed about the set and saw Jacob. For the briefest of moments the monster and Jacob exchanged something, something that came from deep inside. Something he had not felt for a long time.

The monster pulled the tentacle out of Veronica Chaos' mouth and a hole opened on the end. Thick pure white semen, like melted marshmallow, sprayed her in the face.

Jacob's face did not betray any of his true feelings. On the outside he looked indifferent, apathetic. Inside he raged, screamed, and wept. But to any observer he was just another set hand watching a giant monster fuck a porn star.

You can't always get what you want. And, sometimes, you don't even get what you need.

THE SATANIC LITTLE TOASTER

THE PACKAGE finally arrived on a Tuesday afternoon. The small box was wrapped with weathered brown paper splotched with rust-colored stains and bound with frayed twine. It stank of monkey shit.

Paul Goodin eagerly signed for the parcel and bid the postman a "good day." He had been awaiting this particular package—this perfect piece for his collection—for what seemed like a very long time.

He carried the box in awe to his living room, set it down, and rushed off for his digital camera. Paul came back and turned the camera's video recording feature on. He aimed it directly at his face.

"Hi everyone, this is Paul again. I'm back for another unboxing. Today's a really special one. The unboxing of Saint Baxter's Model 1-A-1 Toastmaster or, more commonly called, The Devil's Toaster."

He turned the camera to the package.

"In that small, unassuming box is what is rumored to be the most evil and cursed toaster in the world. Owned by some of history's greatest villains. Or at least that's what the seller assured me—that this was the legit one. Is it real or yet another rip-off? Soon we'll find out.

"Before we go on, let's have a brief history lesson for those out there who are unfamiliar with Saint Baxter."

This part would later be spiced up with pictures and video for the blog. His fans expected a certain level of quality from his productions.

"Ordained by the Catholic Church in 1920, he was sent on a mission to Uganda in the summer of the same year. His stated mission was spreading the word of God. Instead, he spread cruelty, rape, torture, venereal disease, and, if some reports are to believed, cannibalism and necrophilia. He used and abused the very people he was sent to save. But the power and purse-strings of the Catholic Church made it impossible to stop his terror.

"Using money that was allotted to humanitarian needs, he lived in the lap of luxury. In 1925, needing to have the most modern home appliances, he bought one of the world's first pop-up toasters—a Model 1-A-1 Toastmaster produced by the Waters General Company, of course.

"While his unwilling subjects suffered, he dined on eggs, bacon, and *toast* every morning. Until that one fateful day in which the natives had had enough. They dragged him from his tent, shoved a spear up his rear-end, cracked open his skull, and—reports claim—ate his brain while he was still alive.

"The Church—never able to admit any wrong-doing—claimed he was martyred by savages while spreading the gospel. Officially, the Church regards him as a great man but history says differently.

"The locals raided his belongings but no one dared touch the toaster. The mechanical—and to them magical—toasting of bread was mojo they did not want to mess with.

"Legend says that the toaster was snatched and sold by a member of the tribe with little morals. The true provenance of the toaster is shrouded in mystery. Rumors say that it passed through the owner-ship of figures as diverse as Dali, Mussolini, Pol Pot, Salman Rushdie, Danzig, Tony Blair, and Jeffrey Dahmer.

"Earlier this year, an anonymous fan of my videos and collection contacted me and claimed to have come into possession of this fabled and, in some circles, feared toaster.

"After agreeing on quite a large amount of money . . .

"—Twenty-thousand dollars to be exact—

". . . the purchase was arranged, and here I have the package. Is it the real deal or will I be burned like so many times before?

"Let's find out!"

Paul placed the camera on the nearby tripod and assessed the package. His address was carefully hand-printed in black ink. No return address, but he really wasn't surprised about that.

He snipped the twine with scissors and carefully tore off the paper wrapping. Beneath that was a cardboard Amazon.com box that the sender had repurposed. Their address blacked out with magic marker.

Paul opened the box and was greeted with a sea of packing peanuts. He dug into them and his hand groped for the box's contents. At first nothing, but then he found the familiar texture of smooth, cool steel. He greedily ripped the toaster from the box, sending packing peanuts flying through the air.

There it was, in his hand, the toaster of Saint Baxter the Cruel. The Devil's Toaster!

"Oh ladies and gentlemen, this may be it. Oh. Oh. Ohhhhh . . ."

He spun the toaster around in his hands inspecting it from all angles. It appeared to be legit. The steel looked appropriately aged. The design was from the classic golden age of toasters.

"As you can see at home, this is indeed an authentic Model 1-A-1. But is this the one I'm looking for? The so-called, most evil toaster ever made?

"Ladies and Gentlemen, I think it is."

Paul held up the toaster so the camera could see where the power-cord met the toaster.

"Here you can see evidence of a power-surge." He pointed to burn marks. "When Dahmer was cooking up a kidney stew, he was making toast as a side-dish. There was a sudden surge in power and the metal got scorched. The ensuing fire alarms and arriving fire department almost got the famed serial-killer caught. He was apprehended by police three months later."

He flipped around the toaster, "On the front you can see several grooves worn into the steel. William Burroughs grooved them there to snort Cocaine during the writing of *Naked Lunch*."

He turned the toaster so the bottom was facing the video camera. "One of the leg-pegs is missing. Max Hardcore was to have lost it in the ass of Sasha Grey. It was never replaced as a testament to free speech.

"And, most importantly, the mark of authenticity that was only present on the first fifty Model 1-A-1's. A tiny swastika."

Next to the manufacture's info there indeed was a tiny swastika and the year, 1925.

"But there is only one way to truly be sure."

Paul picked up the toaster and the camera. He carried them into the kitchen and plugged the appliance in.

"According to records of all previous owners, the toaster burns some . . . particular . . . patterns into bread."

He took out a loaf of bread and loaded one piece into the toasters. He pushed down the lever and the bread began to toast.

"Some previous owners have claimed to see images of their own death, the fall of global powers, and even winning lottery ticket numbers. But there is one image that is said to appear almost always."

The toast popped up and Paul eagerly snatched it out. His excitement overpowered any heat from the hot bread burning his fingers.

First he sniffed the toast.

"Sulfur," he exclaimed.

Then he inspected the toast and a smiled beamed across his face. He held up the slice to the camera and exclaimed, "Behold, the mark of the Devil's Toaster!"

On the bread, burned perfectly clear, much clearer than that bullshit Mother Mary on grilled cheese from a few years back, was an upside down pentagram.

"The most evil toaster in the world!"

Paul never knew what made him obsessively love toasters. Ever since he was a teen, he accumulated the newest and greatest along with the oldest and most classic models. He learned carpentry to better display his collection. His first apartment didn't have a living room, it had a toaster display room.

If he had ever visited a psychiatrist, like so many ex-girlfriends had advised, he would have learned that his obsession stemmed from his mother making toast every morning before fondling him and playing "where's the sailboat?"

But he never did, and his collection amassed. Soon, everything else in his life other than toasters was shut out. No lover (toasters are not a turn-on), no family (all dead), and no friend (toasters are a very boring hobby). But his IT job for the Global Mart headquarters paid his rent and kept him well-fed and financed his one true love. His town-house was meager but it gave him enough space to store his collection. The first floor, barring the kitchen, was the location of one of the world's foremost toaster collection.

It wasn't much of a life but it was a good one.

His toaster collection grew and grew. He started a website and video blog and soon he even had fans. He wasn't alone in his obsession. There were others just like him.

But over the years, being a toaster expert wasn't enough. BinPoppin in San Francisco had a proto-type designed by President Garfield (toast was a little known passion of the twentieth president). Browned4U in Stewartstown (wherever the fuck that was) had a custom model designed by Andy Warhol. It was limited to three—Elton John and Colin Powell owned the other two.

Paul needed something that would set him apart. Something that would make his collection the envy of all others.

The Devil's Toaster was just the thing.

And now the Devil's Toasters belonged to him.

The video camera was now off. He was free to relax and take in the beauty and history of the accursed object.

He spun the appliance around and clutched it close to his chest. He sniffed it and then placed the bread-slots to his mouth. He sucked in deep a century worth of terror and grilled bread.

Paul got hard.

He stood and cradled the toaster like a baby. He walked across the room to the specialty-built display stand—a white Roman column with a glass dome on top.

Paul lifted the glass and placed the Devil's Toaster atop the column. He moved the cord so it wrapped around the toaster. He regarded it and then moved the cord so it draped down the column.

He frowned, shook his head, and moved the cord back to its original position. Paul smiled, nodded, and put the glass dome back.

He stood back and admired his latest acquisition.

———

The first sign something was wrong came the next Tuesday.

While doing his weekly cleaning, Paul noticed that many of his toasters in his display room were suddenly developing rust. This was unusual as he took great care to ensure that his collection stayed in mint condition.

And this was the worst possible time that his collection should take a hit. Paul had spent three days editing his unboxing video and had posted it. Lusting after the comments other jealous collectors would leave. Instead he got:

—Bullshit. Pics or it didn't happen.

—???????????

—FAKE! Don't waste your time.

And, most insultingly;

—TROLL!!!1!1!!!

Paul had no idea why, but his validity as a collector was being called into question. He now owned the rarest and most infamous toaster in the world but no one seemed to care.

———

"So you're sure it's real?" shouted Frank over the music. There was a loud band on stage at Plan B—a shitty little dive in south east Portland. Frank was another toaster collector. His pride and joys were rare limited edition painted models by Damien Hirst and Andrew Goldfarb. Frank was also another frequent contributor to TOASTERSFORUM and occasional delved into the modding scene. Frank once made a toaster that was also capable of generating a Tesla coil. He was the only collector that Paul really held up as an equal.

"Yeah, I'm sure," replied Paul.

The band on stage—The Toasters—kicked into their next song. They had a three-piece horn section and played something called

"Ska." It sounded like circus music but both Frank and Paul were enamored with the band's name. They each bought t-shirts and grabbed another drink at the bar.

"Your pictures were pretty weird," said Frank.

"What do you mean?"

Frank shouted something back but the noise of the band and the roar of the crowd were too much. Paul couldn't hear the response.

They were sipping white wine at Paul's place after the show when the discussion came up again. Frank was admiring Paul's collection, as he always did, when he came to the steel toaster under glass.

"So you really have it," exclaimed Frank when he eyed the Devil's Toaster.

"Of course I do. You saw the video."

"I saw the video but you weren't unboxing this."

"Then what was I?"

"A 2010 Hello Kitty produced by Spectra Merchandisin. Not that limited and the exact opposite of what you'd expect from a video labeled 'Unboxing of the Legendary Devil's Toaster.' A cute joke but a bit weird."

"What . . ." Paul was extremely confused.

"And then you posted all those pictures to the forum. You got on a serious kick with that. Were you drunk or something?"

"What are you talking about? I did no such thing."

"Yeah. You did."

Frank had moved away from the Devil's Toaster and was inspecting the many shelves of Paul's collection. He had seen it all several hundred times before but he still enjoyed inspecting it yet again. Such is the way of collectors.

"Hey, you really need to take better care of these. A bunch are getting some really nasty rust."

But Paul had gone off to his bedroom to grab his laptop. He came back into the living room and pulled up the video on YouTube. He noticed there were a few dozen new comments. All negative.

"I'm getting tired of this. Here's the video that I uploaded."

Paul hit play. Right when the video got to the point that he was taking the toaster out of the box, Frank interjected—

"And that's a Hello Kitty toaster."

Paul was silent at first. On the screen he could very clearly see the video he shot of unpacking the Devil's Toaster.

"No," he calmly stated, "that's the Devil's Toaster."

"I kind of understand why you want to keep the toaster a secret," said Frank, turning away from the computer, "that I get. But why do you want to keep continuing this stupid joke, to my face, that I don't get. All I see on that screen is Hello Kitty. No Satan."

Paul looked at his friend, not sure which one of them was going crazy.

"Come on," said Frank. He gestured to the Devil's Toaster. "I want to make some Pentagram toast."

After Frank left, Paul caught up with the comments on TOASTERS-FORUM and on YouTube. They all called his posts fake. A few even mentioned Hello Kitty—just like Frank.

Paul angrily finished off his glass of wine and poured another. He got out his video camera and shot another video of the Devil's Toaster. He uploaded the video, finished the glass, and poured another.

Ten minutes later the first comment came: "Another fake. Dude, what's with the Hello Kitty?"

He took down the video immediately.

Paul stayed up late drinking.

One week later, the rust problem was getting much worse.

The ten toasters closest to the Devil's Toaster had grown thick brown fuzz. It looked like some kind of strange mold, but when touched, the "fuzz" broke apart into fine metal shavings.

What was strangest about this weird rust was that it grew overnight. While Paul had been having problems with rust lately, his increased cleaning schedule had seemed to take care of the problem. He couldn't believe his eyes when he walked into the room and saw the brown lumps that had been prides of his collection.

The Devil's Toaster, which was surrounded on both sides by the rusted appliances, was fine.

With a heavy heart Paul trashed the rusted toasters. He went to his storage room and picked out replacements for his display. He had no shortage of options. He owned over two thousand unique models.

———

Paul rushed into the kitchen while he did his tie. He had overslept that morning and barely had any time for breakfast. He grabbed the bag of bread from the counter, went to the toaster, and froze.

Sitting next the cherry red Toast-A-Tron 5000 (limited to 10,000 and Paul's preferred model for daily toasting) was the Devil's Toaster.

Paul looked around the kitchen. Was there a break-in? Was he robbed in his sleep? Was the intruder still in his home?

He picked up the Devil's Toaster and carried it to the living room. He put it back on its display and scanned the room. Nothing else seemed to be disturbed. A quick run through of the other rooms of his house revealed nothing wrong and no doors or windows unlocked.

Perplexed, he went back to the kitchen and loaded bread into the toaster. He pushed down on the lever but nothing happened. No familiar hum of power. No happy warm glow.

He pushed the lever up and back down again. Still nothing.

He checked the back of the toaster and the wall plug. Nothing looked wrong.

Damn thing's busted.

He glanced at his watch. There was no time for cooking anything else. Drive-thru it would be.

As he was putting on his jacket and just about to step out the door he heard a *THUD* from the living room. Was the intruder still in his home?

He crept to the living room and immediately noticed one thing out of place.

The Devil's Toaster had fallen on the floor. The glass dome of its display was undisturbed.

"You know the stories," Frank said and took a swig of beer.

"You can't be serious," replied Paul.

Paul had gone over to Frank's to hang out and see his new Toast-erMaster X in action. After some BLT's they retired to the porch and Paul told Frank of all the strange occurrences that had happened to him lately. The rust, the kitchen toaster (and the one he replaced it with) breaking, and the Devil's Toaster winding up in strange places —that morning he awoke to find the toaster in bed next to him on a pillow, just like the horse head in *The Godfather*.

"Come on Frank, you're a smart man. You can't possibly believe the stories. They're just stupid stories. Cool, yes. But stupid."

"I'm just saying that it's *interesting* that you get the, allegedly, most evil and haunted kitchen appliance ever known and then immediately begin to experience strange phenomena."

"True. Interesting—but still stupid. The weird rust is some leakage or mold problem that I don't know about yet. I'm calling for a guy to come a take a look at the house. I'm worried that the mold might be in the walls."

"And the toaster teleportation?"

"Jesus Christ man, listen to yourself. It's not demons. I'm sure of that. What is it? I don't know yet. It's more likely that I have an undi-agnosed sleep walking problem than supernatural intervention."

Frank shrugged. "I'm just saying."

Paul had the video camera on a tripod pointed at the Devil's Toaster. The nightly moving of it had kept up. Paul was certain he wasn't having a problem with intruders and he refused to accept the supernatural explanation. He was determined to get to the bottom of the mystery.

He walked away from the set-up and paused in the doorway. The room was bare but for the pedestal and glass dome that housed the Devil's Toaster. The rust problem had kept up and actually gotten worse. All the pride and joys of his collection—destroyed. The Devil's Toaster, of course, had somehow managed to avoid catching the metal eating rust.

Paul smiled at the camera and left the room with the light on to ensure the best film quality. If the toaster moved again tonight, he was going to get his answer.

The next morning he found the Devil's Toaster in the storage room —his basement that housed the thousands of toasters that made up his collection. Just like all the other nights, there was no sign of a break-in and nothing else was moved.

Paul rushed to the camera and flipped open the side viewer. The camera had recorded the whole night to the SD card.

He hit stop and started playback. He could perfectly see the toaster atop its pedestal. He started scanning though the video. There was no sign of anything out of the ordinary. Around four a.m., the video rippled and the toaster was gone.

Paul rewound and watched closely. It was the same image as before. It looked like a still-frame if not for the clock in the corner counting away the seconds. At 4:11:32 the video blurred and suddenly cut to black. A split second later the image came back.

The glass dome still sat atop the pedestal but the toaster was gone.

He rewound and watched the moment again and again. He watched it a total of ten times—three in slow motion. But he could see no sign of any intruder or any other way the toaster moved.

Simply, one moment it was there and the next it was gone.

"This is really getting out of hand," said Frank as he took in the devastation.

The rust problem had spread to the storage room. Every toaster Paul owned, from the very first one he ever bought—a special edition Batman model that was made to promote the first Tim Burton film—to the plain banged-up stainless steel model owned by G. Gordon Liddy.

All ruined. All eaten away by the rust plague.

Paul looked broken and that was how he felt. When Cindy left him, when his parents were killed by a drunk driver, when his little Pomeranian, Chu-Chu, was tore apart like a squeaky toy by the nextdoor Doberman—none of those moments compared to how empty he felt now.

When he went to bed last night his collection was fine. But when he awoke this morning, every toaster in the storage room had bloomed a fresh coat of rust. After weeping for a good hour, he called Frank.

"You know what I think this is?" said Frank.

Paul didn't respond.

"It's the only toaster that hasn't been damaged," Frank pointed out.

And that was true. Where the rest of Paul's collection had been destroyed, the Devil's Toaster still sat on its podium in the same condition as the day he unboxed it.

"Hey, have you tried to make toast with it lately?" Frank asked.

"No, why?"

"You know the legend, Cobain, Ted Kennedy, Polanski, the toaster sometimes shows people . . . things. So . . . maybe you should make some toast."

They went to the living room and collected the Devil's Toaster and moved it to the kitchen. Paul plugged it in while Frank got the bread.

Frank handed the bag to Paul. "I think you should do this."

Paul nodded, it was his house and his problems. Would the toaster really reveal the source of his problems or predict some future doom? It seemed impossible but so did a lot lately.

He took out a piece, placed it in the slot, and pushed down on the lever. The metal box hummed and he was close enough to feel the pleasant electrical warmth.

The two men waited in silence. Neither daring to speak. Both wondering what, if any, premonition the toaster would foretell.

POP!

Paul reached slowly for the hot bread. He pulled it out and held it so both of them could see what was burned onto the toast.

Frank had been right to wonder. Before, when they had tested the machine, it had scorched a neat pentagram into the bread. But this time it was something very different.

"I don't get it," said Frank. "What is it?"

"It's . . ." He squinted at the image. "It's a toaster."

Burned into the bread was a crude, simple depiction of a toaster.

Paul tried another piece of bread. And another. And another. They all depicted the same thing—a toaster.

Paul's heartbreak was now replaced with confusion.

Frank grabbed a slice. "Let me try."

He put it in the toaster and a short time later it popped up. He pulled it out and burned onto the bread was the same crude, simple image of a toaster.

Paul had lost it and he knew it. Since his collection got ruined he hadn't been able to eat, go to work, or sleep. He hadn't even visited the TOASTERSFORUM—no way could he go back there. Not after he lost complete creditability with them.

He sat on the floor of his living room staring at the Devil's Toaster. It was three a.m. and a thunderstorm raged outside.

Paul had had enough with all the weird shit. He knew the toaster was somehow responsible for it all and tonight he was going to catch it in the act.

That's how he knew he was going crazy. There was no way a toaster could be evil.

He sipped his coffee and listened to the rain and thunder claps outside. Eventually the combination of coffee and the *putt-putt* of rain droplets caught up to him and he had to take a piss.

He went to the bathroom and relieved himself. As he let out a powerful stream of urine (he had been drinking a lot of coffee) the lights went out.

He looked up and cursed as he heard his piss splashing on the floor. He moved back his aim, finished, and zipped up. He groped around the darkness looking for the light switch. When he found it, he flipped it up and down several times. Nothing.

He blindly found the door and opened it. All the lights in the house were off. The storm must have knocked out the power. But then he noticed there was light in the hallway. Coming from the living room was a warm, flickering orange glow.

Paul slowly crept down the hall—his body tense and filled with a desire to flee from whatever was causing that soft glow.

He turned through the doorway and froze.

The Devil's Toaster was sitting in the living room. It was in the center of five perfectly placed candles. A white grainy substance (toxicology would later confirm it was sea salt) connected the candles with a perfect circle and lines inside crisscrossing forming a perfect pentagram.

There was a bright flash of lightning and a thunderclap like a plane crash. Paul's eyes went all bright and starry, momentarily blinded. When his vision came back the toaster was gone. The candle and salt pentagram remained, but the Devil's Toaster had disappeared.

Paul turned around in a panic and something hard and metal hit him on the bridge of his nose. He crumbled to the ground, blinded by pain.

The metal came down again and again. Wave after wave of pain. He could hear something crunching and then a wet smack. Then he heard nothing.

———

The man walked in to the living room. "Anything?"

"Nothing," said the woman. "Not even a TV. Just this toaster I found by the back door." She tossed the bloody toaster onto the ground next to Paul's brain-splattered still-twitching corpse.

The man looked at the salt and candles. "What the fuck is that shit?"

"Don't know," said the woman. "Freak was into some kinda Satan shit. Come on, let's go. This place is giving me the creeps."

Frank was driving back from Paul's funeral. It had just been him and five of Paul's co-workers. The poor guy had nobody else. It was damned depressing.

Paul had been killed during a home invasion. Some meth-head couple did it to four houses on his street. They cut the power, broke in to murder everyone inside and loot the place. The bastards killed twelve people in total. They got dropped by an NRA card-carrying family man and his pistol-grip shotgun on the fifth house.

Frank pulled into his driveway and there was a package on his doorstep. Strange. He wasn't expecting anything.

He picked up the parcel—a small box wrapped in twin and old brown weather-beaten paper. It stank of monkey shit.

HIPSTER HUNTER

(*Screen is black. A loud gong sounds. A quote in white text fades in.*)

Text: It was the best of fucking times; it was the worst of fucking times. – Frank Booth

(*Cut to black. Fade in on an extreme close-up of bright green grass. Camera slowly pans back and we can see a crushed Pabst Blue Ribbon can come into view. We can hear the sound of shoes pounding on pavement. Someone is running.*

Camera cuts to a very skinny man running down a dark alleyway. He is wearing yellow jeans two sizes too small, a Goonies t-shirt, bright red shoes, a pink scarf, and oversized grandmother sunglasses. He is fleeing in terror from something unknown. His outfit is not designed for a quick getaway and he runs with obvious difficulty.

He stumbles over his own feet and falls into a pile of cardboard boxes filled with trash. The camera zooms in on his terrified face turning around. We can see that he has an asymmetrical haircut that covers the right side of his face. There is a bright blond streak through the front of his hair.

Image changes to the wall of the alleyway and a large shadow falling across it. We can't tell much but we can make out the silhouette of a man with a shotgun.

(Close-up of scared boy)

Emo kid: Who are you? What did I ever do to you?

(View from the perspective of the emo kid looking up. There is a man wearing a black leather jacket with a white t-shirt. His hair is slicked back in a style that would be stylish in the nineteen fifties. He bears more than a passing resemblance to the Fonz. Unlike the Fonz, this guy has a shotgun that is pointed straight at the camera.)

Johnny: I'm Johnny. And why you? Because Pabst Blue Ribbon. Fuck that shit.

(POV view from the emo kid. The shotgun is bearing down on him and we can see the deep black abyss of the barrels. Then there's a flash and blast as the shotgun goes off.

Cut to the interior of a church. A couple in they're in their forties are standing, proudly, behind the bride. The father is wearing too tight jeans, flannel, and proudly sporting a long, bushy beard. The mother has denim short-shorts that are pulled up three inches past her belly-button. She also is wearing a baggy Pac-Man t-shirt, black rimmed glasses that take up half her face, and died black shoulder length hair.

The bride, Jenny, is wearing a vintage 1930s pearl white dress. She is a stunningly beautiful woman. She has a giant green Mohawk and multiple lip, nose, eyebrow, and ear piercings.

The camera pans to the groom walking down the aisle. He is tall and hairy, with a long beard. He wears only glasses and an American flag Speedo. His beer gut stretches faded tattoos from his punk past. He is pushing a fixed-gear bike as we walks. He gets to the stage and smiles at the Jenny. She frowns.

Camera cut to the church doors bursting open and Johnny walks in, blasting indiscriminately into the crowd. We see flashes of people's head's exploding and their gut's being torn out. Both of the bride's parents fall to the ground and they are hit. The groom turns to run but he is shot in the back. Jenny holds her hand close to her chest and screams.

Johnny grabs Jenny by the hand and pulls her off the stage. They run out of the church, hand in hand, while Johnny shots anyone that gets in their path.

They leave the building and there is a cherry-red convertible waiting for them outside the church. They hop in and drive off.

Cut to Johnny and Jenny driving, the top of the car down, and the wind in their hair.

Jenny: So where are we going?

Johnny: Down this road. Then Portland, Oregon. Then, who knows.

(The camera pans back and we see the car drive off into the sunset. Screen goes black)

Title Card: ***Hipster Hunter***

(Their car pulls up in front of a music venue. The building is a white warehouse with peeling paint. Muffled dance beats can be heard.

Cut to Johnny and Jenny, still wearing the wedding dress, standing inside by the bar. They are still and their faces' display disbelief. Every person dancing around them is a hipster. The men all have curly mustaches and the girls all wear over-sized glasses. The camera pans to the band on stage that is playing a synth-heavy, dance-beat version of Cyndi Lauper's Girls Just Want to Have Fun.

Cut to Johnny and Jenny starring. Johnny turns, without emotion, and walks off screen. Jenny continues to stare while the band plays. Johnny walks back on with a gas can and starts tossing gasoline onto the bar behind Jenny.

Cut to Johnny and Jenny leaning against their car. The building is up in flames and people are running out, their thrashing bodies engulfed.

A midget in a red petticoat walks backwards across the street, ignoring the fire and screaming. He is waving his hands in the car above his head in some crude form of dancing.)

Midget: Tihsllub lla si siht. Rophatem a lla si siht.

(Cut to the interior of a different bar. It is a smoky dive with a jukebox blaring Buddy Holly in the background. Johnny is playing pinball. He is no longer wearing the leather jacket but we can now see he has a pack of cigarettes rolled up in his t-shirt's sleeve.

Jenny is next to him now wearing black leather pants and a Leftover Crack tank-top. She is a sobbing wreck, pleading with Johnny.)

Jenny: But Johnny, don't you know I love you? You could leave all this behind and really start a new life with me.

Johnny: I have to.

Jenny: But . . . why, Johnny, why?

Johnny: I . . . I just hate them so much.

(Cut to Johnny and Jenny walking on the sidewalk. They are window shopping in a posh district of the city. They walk pass expensive furniture shop after expensive art gallery. They come upon three street punk kids sitting at the corner, pan-handling. There is a large white dog tied to the parking meter next to them. The dog is jumping around, barking, snarling, and snapping an any passerby.)

Street Punk 1: Yo, you got a dollar to spare?

Johnny: No.

Street Punk 1: Any food.

Johnny: No.

Street Punk 1: Oh, OK.

(The dog keeps jumping around barking. The punks are rolling around their heads, too high to notice.)

Jenny: That dog seems angry.

Johnny: The angriest dog in the world.

(Johnny pulls out a Magnum pistol and shoots the street punks so quick that their drug-addled minds and malnourished bodies have no time to react. The dog starts hopping around, even more frantic and barking louder. Johnny shoots the dog.

Cut to side shot of Johnny and Jenny in a diner. They are both eating cherry pie and drinking coffee.

Close up of Johnny's face, staring intently.

Close up of Jenny's face, sad.

Close up of Johnny as he drinks some coffee. Loud slurping sounds.

Close up of Jenny.)

Jenny: I . . .

(Close up of Johnny and he chops down on a forkful of pie. He chews loudly with his mouth open.

Close up of Jenny.)

Jenny: Can't . . .

(Close up of Johnny as he is drinking the coffee and trying to eat pie at the same time. The coffee is pouring down his chin and the pie is getting smeared across his face.

Close up of Jenny.)

Jenny: Keep . . . Doing . . .

(Cut to Johnny on the street, he is on his knees sobbing. He is getting soaked by rain pouring from the sky.

Camera pans and we see Jenny standing with another man. The man is wearing extra tight yellow jeans and a purple wife-beater. His skinny bare arms are covered in obscure band logos from his high school punk days. He is wearing a brown paper bag over his head. He has glasses (but no eyes) and a mustache (but no mouth) drawn on in black magic marker.

Jenny and the Baghead Hipster turn and walk away from the crying Johnny.

Cut to an extreme close-up of static on a television. The white-noise is overwhelming. The camera turns to reveal a cheap motel room. It continues to rotate and we see Johnny sitting on the ragged and stained bed. He is sitting stiffly upright, a white rabbit is in his lap, sleeping. In one hand Johnny holds a sifter of scotch. In the other he has a cigarette that has burned down and is four inches of ash.

The rabbit lifts its head and looks at Johnny.)

Rabbit: Do the locomotion.

(*Cut to the same static again. The camera turns in the same way as before but to reveal a posh basement apartment. The walls are wood paneled and we see a Big Lebowski poster. The camera continues to turn and we see Jenny and the Baghead Hipster sitting on a bed. There is an oxygen tank next to them. Jenny is staring blankly and the Baghead Hipster is kissing her neck. The bag crinkles loudly as he presses it with lust against her neck.*

The Baghead Hipster pulls back, grabs a gas mask connected to the oxygen tank, and takes a deep, raspy, inhale. He unzips his jeans and turns to Jenny.)

The Baghead Hipster: You stay alive, baby. Do it for Van Gogh.

(*Jenny robotically leans over and begins to give him head.*

Cut to POV from inside a car staring out the front windshield. The headlights are illuminating a dark road and we can only see about six feet ahead. Suddenly a long-hair white cat comes into view on the road. The car rolls overtop, the camera shakes, and there's the sound of a bump and a loud "meow."

Cut to Johnny's car pulling up in front of a doughnut shop. We see him get out of the car and follow him inside from view over his shoulder.

Inside, the shop is empty but for the counter girl. She has short cut hair, arms covered in tattoos of birds and nautical stars, and a septum piercing. She looks up from the book she is reading.)

Johnny: Don't you fucking look at me!

(*Johnny reveals that he is carrying his shotgun. He raises it and shoots the woman point-blank in the chest. She goes flying back into the wall behind the counter.*

Close-up of blood being splatter on a pile of maple-bars with bacon on top.

Cut to a bike shop. There are various people shopping. In the back of the shop is a bar with six men sitting at it, ironically dressed in CARE BEARS shirts. They are vomiting into their pint glasses and then drinking it.

Cut to the door bursting open and Johnny coming in, shotgun firing. He takes out a few of the shoppers and then turns his attention to the men at the bar.)

Puker 2: It is not my custom to go where I am not wanted.

(Puker 2 takes a sip of his vomit and Johnny shoots him in the face.

Cut to Johnny standing in the middle of a street, his shotgun slung across his shoulders. He is in front of a small art gallery. The sign in the front window is advertising a special exhibit composed of "found art" that promises to be an "eye-opening examination of gender." Without warning the building explodes. Johnny gives no indication that anything happened. Johnny walks past the camera and an old man riding a lawnmower drives across the screen in front of the burning rubble.

Cut to an outside street fair. There are people everwhere. There are food carts selling strange ethnic fare. Dotting the crowd are a variety of street performers, from carnival barkers on stilts to human statues.

Jenny and the Baghead Hipster are walking hand-in-hand down the street when suddenly there is the sound of shotgun blasts and people running and screaming.

The camera cuts to a low shot of Johnny confidently stepping forward. Wisps of smoke rise from the gun's barrels.)

Johnny: Hey! That's my girl!

(Cut to the Baghead Hipster reaching behind his back and pulling out a handgun. Before he has a chance to fire, his hand is blown clean off.

He crumbles to the ground and Johnny walks up to him. Johnny grabs the paper bag and pulls is off his head. The man beneath looks identical to Johnny.

Cut to the cool Johnny staring down.

Cut to the hipster Johnny staring up.

Cut to the cool Johnny staring down.

Cut to the hipster Johnny staring up.

Cut to the cool Johnny aiming his gun down.

Cut to a distance shot of the cool Johnny firing and the hipster Johnny falling over.

Cut to a blood splattered cool Johnny turning his attention to Jenny. She is splattered in blood to but has a cool smile on her face.

Johnny climbs on top of a nearby Mexican-Korean fusion food cart. Horns and rock guitars suddenly start blaring in the background and Johnny sings Do You Love Me (Now That I Can Dance) *by the Contours. The crowd of people around them begin to dance the Mashed Potato. After the first verse and chorus he hops down to the street and takes Jenny's hands.)*

Johnny: Don't you feel like this has all happened before?

(Camera pans back and the crowd dances and Johnny and Jenny hold hands, staring deeply into each other's eyes. Another person who looks exactly like Johnny but dressed in a bright purple zoot suit walks to Johnny. The stranger reaches inside his coat and pulls out a handgun. He shoots Johnny in the stomach. Johnny crumples to the ground and grips his gut. He rolls in the street moaning. The crowd stops dancing and stares at this stranger.

The new Johnny pulls Jenny out of the car, dips her back, and kisses her deeply. The crowd starts to do the Robot.

Fade to black.)

JINX POEM

When I first saw you,
I thought you
couldn't
be real.
But you are.
A chick with blowjob lips.
And wearing black face.
That's a little weird...
The voodoo dolls don't help the matter.
At the very least you're an obese drag queen,
who sings opera.
If that's what is true,
good for you.
Lost to a time from a bygone error,
an earlier generation,
of minstrel shows and Ganguro.
Seriously . . . you have tits.
Why must you make me
so uncomfortable?

MOTHERFUCKING DINOSAURS: AN ODE TO DINOSAURS ATTACK!

I WANT to tell you about one of my favorite things in the entire world —the DINOSAURS ATTACK! trading card series.

Before I tell you about this I have to explain some background information. Do you remember that Tim Burton movie from the nineties called MARS ATTACKS? That was actually based on a series of art trading cards from the early sixties. It was basically a gory retelling of the novel WAR OF THE WORLDS (one of my top five favorite books of all-time). Topps Cards produced and released it. That's right, the most famous sports card company in the world use to focus on weird art card. They were also responsible for WACKY PACKAGES and GARBAGE PAIL KIDS.

What has been completely forgotten in pop culture is that in 1988, Topps released a sequel to MARS ATTACKS but instead of invaders from another world it was dinosaurs massacring humanity!

What's so cool about the series is that each card tells a story.

It all starts on an orbiting space station that mankind has built. There's a new technology that is a screen that can show any moment in the history of the Earth. The first time the technology is displayed they show the moment of the dinosaur's extinction and we finally find out what killed the dinosaurs. When they turn the on machine, the screen displays evil eyes staring back at the scientists.

All over Earth, time portals open and dinosaurs jump through them and massacre the human populace.

The card series is full of super gory scenes of dinosaurs eating people. A T-Rex attacks a school and eats children. Pterodactyls attack the White House. A husband and wife are impaled on the horns of a triceratops. And a comic book convention is attacked by some unknown dinosaur that enjoys killing nerds.

Each card shows a new gory image of humans being eaten alive in the worst ways possible. Eyeballs popping out, intestines being dragged out, and there's even a sticker (every pack had one sticker) of a parasaurolophus eating a baby out of carriage with the baby's limbs falling out of the dino's mouth.

As an added bonus, it's not just dinosaurs coming through to attack humanity. There are also cards with dino-based movie monsters joining in on the fun. Gorgo and Godzilla both make cameos in the carnage.

Through all the gore the epic story keeps unfolding, the humans on the space station are working to reverse what they did and close the time portals, BUT it turns out that the plans for the machine were actually placed into the minds of humans by the dinosaurs' God. Who is their God? SATAN!!!

That's right, motherfuckers, dinosaurs worship Satan!

Satan tries to bring Hell on Earth, but the humans are able to reverse the technology sucking all the dinosaurs back into their own time which kills all the dinosaurs. This answers the question, what killed the dinosaurs? We did!

These cards and this insane story came out when I was four-years-old and I remember my dad buying me packs of them when I was around six or eight. Staring at these insanely sadistic images of humans dying in the worst ways possible at the claws of dinosaur monsters definitely did something to my brain. DINOSAURS ATTACK! made me into the man I am today who edits hardcore horror for a living.

Now why haven't you heard of them before? That's another interesting story. Remember how I mentioned Burton's MARS ATTACKS! at the beginning? That wasn't the movie he originally wanted to make. He originally intended to make a movie of

DINOSAURS ATTACK! but then a little film called JURASSIC PARK came out and he didn't want to do another dinosaur movie fearing the two would be compared so instead we got MARS ATTACKS!

It's long been a dream of mine to do an official novelization of the cards and I've attempted many times to get the rights to do it but Warner Bros holds the rights and is refusing to do anything with it.

You can look up every card in the set online and I strongly encourage you to do that. A few years ago I bought a case (twenty-four boxes) of the cards on eBay and have been giving them away at readings and events ever since. So the next time you see me, ask me about DINOSAURS ATTACK! and I may have some cards to give you.

The Very Ineffective Haunted House

There's something about people who are failures but refuse to ever give up that I find charming. The idea of someone who is terrible at something but still keeps trying despite the fact that any rational person would have given up long ago is inspiring to me. I know a lot of artists and writers look positively upon their art but I never feel that way about my stories, I can only see their faults but other people seem to like them so I keep writing them. This is another one of those stupid stories and it's about failure and just leaning into that failure.

But instead of it being about a writer who drinks too much and plays with cats all the time it's about a haunted house who only wanted to be an artist.

The Window Shouldn't Be There

This story came directly from a dream. I literally dreamed everything you read. It wasn't really a nightmare (despite how negative the story goes), as I dreamt, I was just enraptured in this simple but terrifying idea of one day noticing that something fundamentally changed about the building you call your home.

I'm sure there are some psychoanalysts out there that may have something to say about this story. If you read this and are one, I would love to hear from you over what the hell my brain was trying to say to me.

Ten Secrets to Survival Clickers Don't Want You to Know - They Really Hate Number Six

In 2014 writer J.F. Gonzalez untimely passed away from complications due to cancer. He was an instrumental force for two generations of horror writers and fans. I was one of them. The first time I read his seminal hardcore horror novel, SURVIVOR, it blew my mind. I was fortunate enough to work with him on several projects years later as I reprinted many of his books through the Eraserhead Press imprint, Deadite Press.

To honor Gonzalez, Brian Keene edited an anthology in tribute to him and I was one of the many creative voices who were invited to contribute. Instead of writing a story in his hardcore horror world (which many would have expected of me), I instead went to his work of clickers—giant insect/crab/scorpion monsters who invade from the oceans.

I went to the bar to brainstorm ideas and this is the one that I was happiest with, it's a play on the concept of click bait online articles (get it? Clickers? Click bait?).

I like to think this story would have made him laugh.

How I Got a MY LITTLE PONY Tattoo

This is one of the most personal stories I've ever written but not in the ways that most authors mean when they say that. This isn't some deep exploration of my personal feelings but a story about one of the absolute worst experiences of my entire life.

This story is about bed bugs.

A few years ago I lived in downtown Portland and the apartment building got infested with them. It was one of the worst experiences of my entire life. I still have the literal scars on my body from them.

This story is barely fictional. Almost everything in here actually happened to me in real life. The biggest change is that this story doesn't have bed bugs. It has...well, you'll see...

The GG Effect

Emma Johnson of Weirdpunk Books started her press with an anthology tribute to the notorious punk asshole GG Allin. She invited me to contribute but I have to admit that I hate GG Allin. I've been involved in the punk scene since I was fourteen but I come from the political DIY end. My idols were the Clash, Crass, Dead Kennedys, Aus-Rotten, and Choking Victim/Leftover Crack. To me punk is interchangeable with political protests, feminism, worker's rights, and fighting fascists in the streets. To say that I don't relate to GG Allin (who was convicted of sexual assault) is a vast understatement.

But I had this great idea. A way to talk about how awful that piece of shit excuse for humanity was in a positive way.

The Dog Who Stared

When I was a kid I had this awesome dog. He was a West Highland Terrier aka a Westie. I named him Spock because he had these giant pointed ears. He was just an absolutely ridiculous dog that was full of life and despite his tiny stature was sure he could take down a bear. And you know what? I believe that he could.

But he had this weird thing that he liked to do. He would go out into the yard, sit down, and just stare into the sky. He wasn't looking at a bird or a squirrel or anything else. He just liked to stare straight into the sky. I always wondered what he was looking at that I couldn't see.

The Most Accomplished Crackhead in the World

Bizarro author Kevin Shamel (ROTTEN LITTLE ANIMALS and ISLAND OF THE SUPER PEOPLE) use to work in the Eraserhead Press offices before he got married and moved to Australia. While he worked there he and I would spend lots of time talking about all sorts of stuff. He would tell me about was his adventurous and, at times, his sordid past.

One thing he'd tell me about that really fascinated me was his past experience with hard drugs—something I have zero experience with (I stick to booze, weed, and the occasion psychedelic). In particular his description of crack really stuck with me. He described it as being filled with motivation and energy but all you do with it is unless and stupid shit.

That, in a weird way, excited my imagination. What could be something positive someone could do with crack?

I've Seen Enough Hentai to Know Where This is Going

I spend a lot of time online doing things like looking at memes and reading Reddit. I also have spent a lot of the past two years battling depression issues. While I love talking about first, the second isn't really something I like to address to others.

This story is my attempt to combine both concepts. It's about how even when you think you've got everything you want it's just not enough to fix those dark and negative feelings inside.

On a less depressing note—the porn star in the first scene, Veronica Chaos, is a real person and a very good friend of mine. In real life she doesn't fuck monsters, she fucks a ventriloquist dummy (seriously).

The Satanic Little Toaster

There's this GIF that goes around that was taken from a segment from THE TODAY SHOW about a haunted toaster. It shows this old woman whose toaster burns the toast with the words "Satan Lives." It fucking cracks me up!

That really stupid internet meme just infected my brain. The idea of a common kitchen appliance being a direct path to the dark lord was just something I could not shake. So I wrote this piece of extremely stupid horror.

A note about the title – It's a play on the children's animated movie, THE BRAVE LITTLE TOASTER. According to my Mom, I use to watch that movie on repeat when I was a little kid but I have no memory of it. It seems every time I see her she brings it up and she can't believe I don't remember the movie. But it must have left some impression on me because I think toasters are pretty cool.

Hipster Hunter

Cameron Pierce edited a tribute anthology to David Lynch and he invited me to contribute. I jumped at the chance, mostly because I'm not a fan of Lynch. I know, I know, most of you reading this probably love him but I find him to be an extremely uneven director. At his best he's a surreal visionary but at his worst he is pretentious hipster bullshit. In this story I tried to pay tribute to both sides of his career.

Fun fact – I have references to all ten of his films, to multiple TV shows he worked on, and multiple short films.

See if you can spot them all!

It seems I keep writing stories for tribute anthologies about people I dislike.

Jinx Poem

At one point Cameron Pierce had this brilliant idea of doing an anthology of 150 different authors doing poems on the original 150 different Pokémon from the first games (Red and Blue). I loved this idea so much and I wished that it had happened but unfortunately a few of the major authors pulled out and there was a complete shit show with others and it all fell apart. It still frustrates me that this project never came to light.

I had already written may poem when the all the shit hit the fan. I had requested what is easily the most offensive Pokémon ever designed and my poem is kinda based around seeing how uncomfortable the creature design is to a Western audience.

ACKNOWLEDGEMENTS

This collection is a culmination of good times and bad times. It's about the bullshit that we call life and the little things that get us through and the little things that drag us down.

None of these stories would exist without the help, friendship, and constant irrational faith that the following people give me:

Liz Canup, Christoph Paul, Leza Cantoral, Cameron Pierce, Rose O'Keefe, Carlton Mellick III, Kevin L. Donihe, Brian Keene, John Skipp, J. David Osbourne, Jeremy Robert Johnson, Skwert, J. F. Gonzalez (RIP), Veronica Chaos, David Agranoff, Emma Johnson, Garrett Cook, Whitney Streed, Dave Brockie (RIP), Shane McKenzie, Chester Knebel, Edward Lee, MC Devlin, Chrissy Horchheimer, Godzilla, Night Gaunts, Christine Morgan, Jack Ketchum (RIP), Cody Goodfellow, William Shatner, Miss Spooky, Night Gaunts, that dude that got me high outside of the bar that one time, Andrew Goldfarb, Pedro Proença, Angie Molinar, Ryan Harding, Nick Mamatas, and a shit ton of other people I'm probably going to be embarrassed that I forgot.

Extra special thanks and cuddles to:

Squishy, V.P., Gomez, Natasha, and Lovecraft (RIP)

Fuck off to:

You know who you are.

ABOUT THE AUTHOR

JEFF BURK is the cult favorite author of SHATNERQUAKE, SUPER GIANT MONSTER TIME, CRIPPLE WOLF, and SHAT-NERQUEST. He is also the Head Editor of ERASERHEAD PRESS' horror imprint, DEADITE PRESS and the host of the JEFF ATTACKS podcast.

Born in the Pennsylvania backwoods, he was raised on a steady diet of Godzilla, Star Trek, and EC Comics. He now resides in Portland, Oregon. His influences include sleep deprivation, comic books, drugs, magick, and kittens.

author photo drawing by Carlton Mellick III

CLASH

WE PUT THE **LIT** IN LITERARY

ALSO BY CLASH BOOKS

DARK MOONS RISING IN A STARLESS NIGHT by Mame Bougouma Diene

IF YOU DIED TOMORROW I WOULD EAT YOUR CORPSE by Wrath James White

THE ANARCHIST KOSHER COOKBOOK by Maxwell Bauman

HORROR FILM POEMS by Christoph Paul

THIS BOOK IS BROUGHT TO YOU BY MY STUDENT LOANS by Megan Kaleita

GIRL LIKE A BOMB by Autumn Christian

HE HAS MANY NAMES by Drew Chial

SEQUELLAND by Jay Clayton-Joslin

CLASH MAGAZINE: Issue #1

TRAGEDY QUEENS: STORIES INSPIRED BY LANA DEL REY & SYLVIA PLATH edited by Leza Cantoral

THIS BOOK AIN'T NUTTIN TO FUCK WITH: A WU-TANG TRIBUTE ANTHOLOGY edited by Christoph Paul & Grant Wamack

WALK HAND IN HAND INTO EXTINCTION: STORIES INSPIRED BY TRUE DETECTIVE edited by Christoph Paul & Leza Cantoral